THE MAVERICK'S
BABY
ARRANGEMENT

THE MAVERICK'S BABY ARRANGEMENT

KATHY DOUGLASS

MILLS & BOON

First published in Great Britain 2020
by Mills & Boon, an imprint of HarperCollins*Publishers*
1 London Bridge Street, London, SE1 9GF

Large Print edition 2020

© 2020 Harlequin Books S.A.

Special thanks and acknowledgement are given to
Kathy Douglass for her contribution to the
Montana Mavericks: What Happened to Beatrix? miniseries.

ISBN: 978-0-263-08517-4

MIX
Paper from
responsible sources
FSC™ C007454

This book is produced from independently certified FSC™ paper to ensure responsible forest management. For more information visit www.harpercollins.co.uk/green.

Printed and bound in Great Britain
by CPI Group (UK) Ltd, Croydon, CR0 4YY

This book is dedicated with love
to my wonderful husband and sons.
Each day with you is better
than the one before.

Chapter One

Brittany Brandt double-checked the contents of her tan leather satchel, making sure she had everything she needed before snapping it shut. She closed her eyes, inhaled deeply then slowly blew out her breath, envisioning a successful outcome to her meeting with Daniel Dubois. Other planners at Bronco Hills Elite Parties, the event-planning firm where she'd been employed for the past several months, had been reluctant to take him on when he'd hired the firm to plan an important dinner party. While the others had cowered in fear, Brittany had stepped forward. She wasn't afraid of a challenge—or of a man rumored to be impossible to please.

Besides, organizing his party was part of her master plan to advance her career and earn a promotion to partner. Shying away from hard situations and difficult clients wasn't going to help her accomplish that goal. Showing her bosses and the upper crust of Bronco, Montana, what she was capable of doing would.

She'd been fully aware that Mr. Dubois wouldn't be the easiest person to work with before she'd volunteered to take on the job. The trail of other event planners who'd scurried away from Bronco with their tails between their legs made that abundantly clear. Everybody knew that BHE wasn't his first event planner. Or second, for that matter. Originally, he'd hired a firm from L.A. with a reputation of catering to celebrities. They hadn't lasted long. Next, he'd hired a big-name firm out of Chicago. They'd come and gone even more quickly. There'd also been some firm from New York, but their tenure had been so short they were hardly worth mentioning. He'd finally decided to toss the local firm a bone as if doing BHE a favor.

Others might be offended by being a last choice, but not Brittany. In fact, to her, the failure of the other firms was a good thing. Once she pulled off the event—and she had no doubt she *would* pull it off in spectacular fashion—the Who's Who in town would take notice of her and beat a path to her firm, requesting to work with her specifically. Cornelius Taylor, the patriarch of the richest family in Bronco, would certainly be impressed enough to hire her. She'd pitched her idea of the Denim and Diamonds fundraiser to raise money for programs to aid low-income families in Bronco to him, but so far he hadn't been persuaded. Although she'd put the idea on the back burner temporarily, she wouldn't give up on it. But right now, she needed to focus on creating a memorable dinner party for Mr. Dubois.

Opening her eyes, she grabbed her satchel and purse, strode from her office and into the main area of the firm. Rachel, the assistant Brittany shared with two other planners, looked up from her desk and smiled. "Heading off to your meeting with Mr. Dubois?"

"Yes."

Rachel pretended to shiver in fear. "You're braver than I am."

"He's just a man."

"A man who has chased off three firms already."

Brittany waved a hand in dismissal. "I'm made of sterner stuff. Plus, they weren't as creative as I am. Or as determined. There's no way I'm going to run away in fear from any man."

"Knowing you, you'll have him eating out of your hand before the meeting is over."

"I won't go that far. I know he's no pushover. But remember, I'm the oldest of five children. I have experience dealing with stubborn and demanding people. Trust me, nobody is more unreasonable than a two-year-old hopped up on sugar at bedtime."

Rachel laughed. "I've seen the man, albeit

from a distance. There's nothing childish about his looks."

Brittany already knew that. Although she had yet to meet Daniel in person, she'd seen pictures of him in gossip rags and business magazines. The creativity she used in her job failed her when it came to describing Daniel Dubois. The best she could do was *tall, dark and handsome.* Cliché as it was, the saying fit him to a T. He had a face designed to make a woman's heart beat faster and a muscular body that had Brittany imagining things she shouldn't if she wanted him as a client. In short, he was six feet of deliciousness.

"No, there isn't. But since his personality isn't nearly as appealing as his looks, I'd better get going. The last thing I want to do is get on his bad side by being late."

"From what I can see, the man doesn't have a bad side," Rachel quipped.

Brittany laughed then left.

Daniel Dubois was a very wealthy horse rancher and his lifestyle reflected that. He owned a magnificent property in the exclusive section of Bronco Heights.

Two hours north of Billings, Bronco was actually two cities: Bronco Heights where the incredibly rich people resided and Bronco Valley where the regular folks lived. Bronco Heights was consistently included on lists of the country's best places to live while Bronco Valley's claim to fame was as a popular tourist destination.

As Brittany drove through the town, she passed by the business district. Exclusive boutiques, a high-end jewelry store and DJ's Deluxe upscale barbecue restaurant lined the pristine streets. Shoppers strolled down the wide walks, enjoying the beautiful late-summer day.

After a relaxing ride, Brittany reached the winding road that lead to the Dubois mansion. Signaling, although there was no traffic behind her, she drove the nearly mile-long private road to his estate. The sprawling property was nothing short of magnificent and she slowed to take it all in.

The ranch had an air of serenity that only nature could provide. She was slightly nervous about her upcoming meeting and, with each breath she took, she felt more tranquil. In the distance, deer and elk meandered between the trees as if they, too, were at peace. Mountains soared in the background, reaching toward the wide sky. Given the amount of money Dubois had, she wasn't surprised by the grandeur. What was surprising were the numerous small cabins she spotted in the distance. She briefly wondered what they were for and then dismissed the thought as unimportant. She was here to plan his dinner. Nothing else about Daniel Dubois was her concern.

Brittany parked her car at the end of the long circular drive, using the walk to the portico to prepare herself mentally for the meeting.

As she neared the covered walkway, she spotted Malone, the cook for one of Bronco's established families—the Abernathys—coming out the front door. Although she didn't know him very well, she liked the older man and called out a greeting to him. He spun around and looked at her. His face flushed momentarily before the color drained from it, leaving him pasty white. He appeared guilty, although she couldn't imagine why.

"Hi. Funny seeing you here," she said with a smile.

"Yes. Well." Clearly flustered, he took a deep breath. "I've been working for the Abernathys for more than twenty years. And I like my job and am very loyal to them."

"Of course." Where was all this going? She'd only been making small talk. She certainly didn't expect an accounting of the man's time or an explanation of his presence.

"I didn't know that Mr. Dubois had invited me out here to try and hire me away from the Abernathys. Had I known that, I would have saved both his time and mine."

Brittany nodded as the older man continued on his way. Apparently, loyalty didn't mean anything to Daniel Dubois. If he didn't expect people to be loyal to their employers, he surely wouldn't regard loyalty to his employees as something that he owed. She briefly wondered if he applied that same attitude to personal relationships then brushed the ridiculous thought aside. The only relationship she wanted with him was a business one. One where contracts would be signed and expectations clearly spelled out, not one where her heart was on the line.

Not that she was at risk of losing her heart to him—or anyone else, for that matter. She was a career woman through and through. Marriage and kids weren't part of her five-year plan.

Brittany reached the front door and rang the bell. The sound of chimes filtered through the open windows and continued for several seconds until the melody finished. A moment later, the door swung open, revealing a uniformed woman who appeared a few years older than Brittany's own thirty-three. The woman introduced herself as Marta, Daniels's housekeeper, then she ushered Brittany inside and closed the heavy wooden door behind them.

"I'm Brittany Brandt."

Marta smiled. "Welcome. You're right on time, which will please Mr. Dubois. He'll be right with you. He'll meet with you in the study."

Brittany followed the woman through the entry, through an impressive living room and several equally large rooms, before coming to a closed carved-mahogany door. Marta opened the door and waved Brittany inside. "Would you like a drink? The cook just made fresh lemonade."

"Thank you, no. I'll just wait for Mr. Dubois."

"Okay." Marta left, closing the door behind her.

Alone, Brittany took the opportunity to look around, trying to get a feel of Daniel's style. In her experience, clients often could not put their likes or dislikes into words. She couldn't count the number of times someone had told her they knew what they liked when they saw it. Which was fine when it came to deciding which dress to buy. It wasn't as helpful when putting together a special event.

Though she'd only glimpsed the other rooms, adding that bit of knowledge to her quick study of this room revealed that his taste ran toward the masculine and Western. And exceedingly expensive. She ran her hand across a carved horse and rider sitting on the corner of his massive desk then crossed the room to the far wall where a built-in cabinet was filled with trophies for horse breeding. Several awards and commendations from civic organizations were there, as well. Beside the trophy case was a prominently displayed framed letter thanking Mr. Dubois for his ongoing generous contributions to their organization supporting mental health. Another letter thanked him for funding the Francine Dubois scholarship. She briefly wondered whether the woman was his mother.

Apparently, he was a charitable man, which was a mark in his favor. He might be demanding, but clearly he cared about those who were less fortunate than he was. A believer in giving to others whenever she could, Brittany's opinion of Daniel Dubois rose several notches. Not enough to put up with any nonsense from him, but enough to give him the benefit of the doubt when necessary.

But something was missing in the room. There were no personal items. No photos of people he loved. People who were important to him. She thought it best to keep business and personal lives separate, but this was his *home* office. Surely, a personal item here or there would be acceptable. Come to think of it, she hadn't glimpsed anything personal in the other rooms, either. Curiouser and curiouser.

She heard the door open and she turned. Daniel Dubois stepped into the room. Brittany took one look at him and barely managed to stifle a gasp. The magazines hadn't done him justice. They'd completely failed at capturing his good looks. Daniel Dubois was absolutely stunning.

He had the kind of chiseled features that

could make women swoon. Even her knees weakened for a moment before she forced herself to stay upright. His light brown skin was unmarred by the slightest blemish and his dark brown eyes, rimmed by thick soot eyelashes, were filled with intelligence. With his looks, he could make a fortune as a male model.

More than great looks, he had a commanding presence. No doubt he'd dominate any room he entered. He smiled as he crossed the room to shake her hand and her stomach took a foolish tumble. *No way.* He was a client. She couldn't allow herself to feel the slightest attraction to him.

"Thank you for waiting."

"No problem." As she shook his hand, she felt the calluses on his palm. Daniel Dubois wasn't some rich guy dabbling in ranching until something else drew his attention. He worked his ranch. Impressive.

After declining his offer of a beverage, she let him lead her to a seating area in front of a wall of floor-to-ceiling windows. The drapes had been pulled back, revealing a view of the ranch that went on forever. From this vantage point, she could see all the way to a babbling brook about twenty yards away. Shrubs and purple-and-yellow wildflowers billowed in the breeze and a few deer drank from the water As dedicated as she was to her work, she'd have to use all of her discipline to not be distracted by the beauty the windows revealed.

Once they were seated, her on the brown leather sofa and him on a coordinating chair beside her, she opened her notebook and took out a pen. She preferred the old-fashioned method of taking notes when meeting with clients. It was more personal and didn't create the artificial distance a computer did.

"So, tell me about your event. What do you envision? What are your goals?"

He leaned against the back of his chair, stretched his long legs in front of him and crossed his ankles. Dressed in comfortable jeans that had been faded over time and a chambray shirt that stretched across his muscular chest and shoulders, he looked at ease. But given his reputation, she knew his mind was sharp and that he wouldn't miss a trick.

"Did you notice the cabins in the distance while you were driving in?"

"Yes. They're lovely."

"Those are guest cabins. I plan to turn a part of my ranch into a dude ranch. A top-of-the-line resort worthy of Bronco Heights and serving an exclusive clientele. I've been in business long enough to know that community buy-in is important to any business. Although there is a lot of land between me and my neighbors, I want them to feel comfortable with what I'm about to do with my property."

"That's a good idea."

"That's where you come in. I want to have a dinner for the leading families and community leaders in Bronco to inform them about the resort. I'll distribute information packets as well as answer any questions they may have."

Brittany nodded. She admired the way he

planned to take the proverbial bull by the horn. As a newcomer to town, he would be subject to a lot of suspicion by the old-moneyed folk who at times could be a bit insular. He struck her as someone who wouldn't be cowed and who'd soon earn everyone's respect.

He glanced at her and his beautiful smile faded. "Why do you think you're qualified for a job that other firms were incapable of handling?"

Brittany was momentarily stunned by the abrupt change from charming man to cold businessman, but she shifted gears, as well. Now that the pleasantries were over, it was down to business. "I can't say why the others failed, because I'm not acquainted with them. What I can tell you is that I'm good at my job. Very good. You strike me as someone who knows what he's doing, so I'm sure you've already asked about me."

"I have."

"Then you know I have an excellent reputation."

"I've heard good things. But I also know that you've only been with Bronco Heights Elite Parties for a few months. Before that you worked at that ghost-hunting company." He shook his head, making it obvious what he thought of *that* business. "All told, you don't have very much experience."

"I can see how you would believe that."

"It's not a belief. It's a fact."

She'd give him that. "The people you hired before had experience, right?"

"Yes."

"How'd that work out for you?"

His eyes narrowed. Obviously, he didn't like being challenged.

Smiling internally, she continued. "They weren't able to deliver. Clearly, a long résumé doesn't guarantee ability or a successful outcome. You should consider my natural assets." He raised an eyebrow and she realized how suggestive that comment sounded. Rather than try to clean it up and thereby prolong the uncomfortable moment, she soldiered on. "I have skills that can't be taught.

I can arrange a dinner party that your guests will be buzzing about for months. And I guarantee they'll be lining up for invitations to your next dinner party while those unfortunate enough to have been left off the guest list try to wrangle invitations to your next event. More than that, it'll drum up interest and support for your resort."

"You're pretty sure of yourself."

"I know what I can do."

He nodded, as if impressed. "Do you have time to see the ranch? If you're going to be organizing this function, it would be helpful for you to have a look around."

"I have time." She'd cleared the afternoon for the express purpose of getting to know him.

"Okay. There are a few places we can only reach by horseback, so I'll have to settle with describing them to you."

"Why? I can ride."

One side of his lips lifted in a sexy half smile that had her toes curling in her boots.

She forced them straight. She didn't get involved with clients.

"Really? In that case, let's take the horses."

"Yes. Let's."

He stood and held out his hand to her. Pleasantly surprised by the gesture, she placed her hand in his and rose. He led her from his office and through the magnificent house. The rooms were spacious, airy and exquisitely decorated, if a little masculine for her taste. But then there wasn't a Mrs. Dubois in the picture to soften the décor. Or the man.

They walked through a long hallway where gorgeous paintings hung from the dark-paneled wall. She would have liked to slow down to get a better look at the artwork, but he was on a mission. Nearly half a foot shorter, she couldn't keep up with his long strides.

They exited through a door and stepped into the warm air. She inhaled the scent of wildflowers and freshly mowed grass. The view from here was even better than the one from his office, showing a property more expansive than she'd thought. A paved path led from the door into two directions. One led to a small pond. The other—the one they took—led to the stables.

A man approached them as they stepped inside, pulling his cowboy hat from his head when he saw her. "Good afternoon, Mr. Dubois. Ma'am."

"Hi," Brittany said.

"I'm going to take Ms. Brandt on a ride around the ranch, Jerry. Would you saddle Sugar Cookie for her?"

"Right away," he said and then ambled away.

"Sugar Cookie?" Brittany asked. He didn't strike her as the kind of man who'd give a horse such a fanciful name.

"I didn't choose it," he said quickly, as if his man card was in danger of being revoked. "The previous owner's daughter named her that."

"I think it's sweet."

He snorted and strode to a stall where a gorgeous stallion waited. In under a minute, he'd saddled the horse and led it to where Brittany waited. The groom returned with Sugar Cookie and stepped up beside Brittany to help her mount.

"I'll do that," Daniel said.

"Okay," Jerry said and walked away.

Before Brittany could tell Daniel that she was perfectly capable of mounting the horse on her own, he was beside her. When he gently put his hands on her waist and, her voice abandoned her as he lifted her into the saddle. She inhaled and she was instantly surrounded by his masculine scent. Her heart beat a little faster and the blood raced through her veins. Then he adjusted her stirrups. When he turned his back and returned to his own horse she blew out a shaky breath and wiped her hand across her suddenly damp brow.

How many times did she have to remind herself that she didn't get involved with clients? She'd never struggled this hard to keep business and personal separate. Hopefully, this was a temporary problem.

She twisted in her seat, getting comfortable in the saddle. If she'd known ahead of time that she'd be riding a horse, she would have worn jeans and a T-shirt instead of the high-waisted black pants and pink-and-white chiffon blouse. But since this was the opportunity to get to know Daniel better, she wouldn't complain. Besides, her parents owned a large dry-cleaning business, so getting her clothes cleaned wouldn't be a hassle.

Daniel swung up onto his stallion and led them out of the stable and into the pasture. Without the slightest hesitation, he started off across the large expanse of grass. He went slowly at first, as if not believing she could really ride. She'd grown up in Montana. Of course she could ride.

Apparently satisfied that she knew what she was doing, he sped up. She tried to keep her eyes on the beautiful scenery, but they kept drifting to Daniel's muscular body. He looked so fine riding on his stallion that her mouth began to water.

She was in unchartered territory here. Normally she had laser focus on work. Now the dinner was the farthest thing on her mind. The only thing she could concentrate on was the very sexy Daniel Dubois. If she didn't get her wayward mind under control and tamp down on her attraction, she was going to be in deep trouble.

Chapter Two

Daniel glanced at Brittany. She was smiling broadly, her beautiful brown eyes gleaming with excitement, her cheeks glowing. What in the world had possessed him to invite her to go riding with him? It certainly hadn't been part of the plan when he'd set up the meeting. If he had stuck to his agenda, she would be on her way back to her office and he would be repairing fences or one of the many other tasks he'd scheduled for today. Yet, here they were.

He had to admit that he'd enjoyed sparring with her. She wasn't afraid to voice her opinion, something he admired. The last thing he wanted was to do business with someone who didn't stand up to him. Weak people generally made bad employees and even worse partners. And if she was going to work with him on this party, they'd be partners, so it made sense to get to know each other better.

After they'd accomplished everything they'd needed to in his office, he'd been about to bring the meeting to a close. Then she'd crossed her legs and his mind had begun to wander to places that had nothing to do with business. Her sweet scent had wafted over to him, tying him up in knots, and his good sense had deserted him.

So instead of saying goodbye, he'd invited her for a tour. Now they were galloping across the ranch to one of his favorite spots. An argument could be made that it would help if she saw more of his land and got the complete picture of what he planned to do. But it wasn't essential to her role as party planner. Besides, the waterfall wouldn't be accessible to the resort guests, so there'd been no real reason to bring her here. But still, he'd wanted to share this spot with her. To see her reaction. If her quiet gasp was anything to go by, she was getting just as much pleasure from her surroundings as he always did.

Bringing his horse to a stop, he dismounted. He was about to help Brittany when she expertly got off her horse on her own. They looped the horses' reins around a tree branch then stood side by side.

"This is beautiful. How many acres do you own?"

"Two hundred and sixty."

"Wow." She turned in a slow circle and, when her back was to him, his eyes strayed to her round bottom. He'd tried not to notice the way her pants fit, but he was still a man. Ignoring such an enticing sight was something he wasn't equipped to do.

"That's what I thought when I found this spread. I rode over every acre before deciding that this was the perfect place for my horse ranch. Then I had to find the right place to build my house. I wanted easy access to my home from the road, but I want privacy from the guests. It's a balancing act."

"One that you've handled very well." She gave him the once-over, taking him in from boots to hat before her eyes met his. "So why did you bring me out here on this ride? You could have told me about your ranch just as easily while we were sitting in your office."

The way her eyes held his was impressive. Most people avoided prolonged eye contact. And they certainly didn't challenge him. "Seeing it for yourself is better than any description I could have given."

"So you're admitting to a weakness?"

"I wouldn't exactly call it that. As the saying goes, a picture is worth a thousand words."

She grinned and the picture she presented would need more than a thousand words to describe. Or perhaps not. Maybe only one was necessary. *Stunning.*

Brittany Brandt was absolutely stunning. He frowned. Her appearance was the last thing he should be thinking about. His plate was already overflowing without adding a woman to the mix. Not that he was considering doing that. Admiring Brittany's beauty and spunk was miles away from becoming romantically involved with her. But with that smile lighting her face and the joy radiating from her every pore, given the right motivation and opportunity, he would cross that distance in a heartbeat.

"Another reason I brought you out here," he continued, pulling his mind back to business, "is so you can get the feel of the land. Smell the fresh air. Soak in the atmosphere."

She stared at him for a long moment and he wondered if he'd waxed too poetic. He frowned. Since when did he doubt himself? Brittany's presence was definitely affecting him—and not in a good way. She had managed to knock him off-kilter. He didn't like the feeling.

"I'll be able to use this experience to bring the party to life."

"Then I succeeded."

"Trust me, this party is going to achieve each of your goals."

He blew out a breath. "I hope so. I'm new to Bronco. I've only been here a year and people have been slow to warm up to me. Not that it was entirely unexpected. I bought one of the biggest ranches in the area. This is prime real estate that no doubt one of the old-timers wanted for one of his kids. That I own a horse ranch in the middle of cattle country didn't help. I don't want to be enemies with my neighbors. I would like to have cordial relationships with all of them if possible."

Brittany smirked. "Quiet as it's kept, not all of your neighbors get along with each other. There's a new money versus old money dynamic in Bronco Heights. Then there's the wealthy Bronco Heights versus the middle-class Bronco Valley divide. City council meetings are boisterous, to say the least. I predict that one day the fights won't stop with words."

"I hope it doesn't come to that."

"My point is twofold. First, getting along with all of your neighbors might be a pipe dream. Honestly, I'm not sure it's wise to have some of them in a room at the same time. Second, you're not the only one on the receiving end of the cold shoulder."

"I don't know if that's better or worse," he said with a laugh.

She laughed with him. "Of course, with an expert like me on your side, someone local who knows all the players, the impossible will be made possible."

"Is that right?" Daniel took a step closer to her and, although her eyes widened, she didn't back away. He wasn't sure whether that was good or bad. Did she feel the attraction between them? Did she share the same yearning to close the distance separating them? To touch? She nibbled on her full bottom lip, mesmerizing him.

Suddenly a bird squawked overhead, breaking the spell, and Daniel's senses returned.

What was wrong with him? This was a business meeting, not a date. He pointed to several boulders shaded by a large oak tree, where they could sit and talk.

She walked beside him. After they sat, she

turned to him. "Just tell me what you envision. I know what you *want*. You want the support of the community. Tell me what you *see*. What do you visualize this dinner looking like? Paint a picture for me."

Art was never his strong suit. In fact, he didn't have a gift for any of the softer subjects like music, literature or the like. Math. Science. That's where he'd excelled. After earning a Ph.D. in mechanical engineering from MIT, he and his best friend, who'd gotten an MBA from Harvard, had started a bioengineering company that was a leader in genetic testing. They'd taken the company public six years ago and made more money than either of them had ever dared to dream. Two years ago, Daniel had resigned as CEO. He still owned stock in the company and was on the board of directors, but he was no longer involved in day-to-day operations. Last year, he'd moved from Texas to Montana to live his dream of ranching and owning an exclusive dude ranch. His background in genetics came in handy when it came to breeding horses and he was becoming successful and making a name for himself in the industry.

Stephanos Dimitry, his former partner, hadn't understood why Daniel had wanted to leave, but as a good friend, had wished him well. He'd also promised to be Daniel's first guest once the resort was up and running.

"Well?" she prompted when he just sat there like a bump on a log.

"I want my dinner guests to see the good in what I'm doing. I want them to see the positive impact the resort will have on the entire community. I want them to feel invested in the success of the business."

"I can do all of that for you. And more. Believe me when I tell you that I'm not simply the best person for the job. I'm the only person."

His phone rang before he could comment. He glanced at the screen then answered the call. "Mr. Dubois?" The woman's voice trembled, striking fear in Daniel's heart.

"Yes? Is everything okay?" Worry made

his voice sharp. Brittany raised an eyebrow but remained silent.

"No. I have to leave. I have a family emergency."

"Leave? When?" He jumped to his feet.

"Now."

He ran across the grass. Brittany, as if sensing something was wrong, was right behind him. "I'm on my way back to the house. I'll be there in twenty minutes. I expect to see you when I get there."

"I—" She sputtered as he ended the call. He didn't want to waste time having a phone conversation; they needed to speak in person.

He grabbed Lightning's reins and hopped on his back. "I need to get home."

"Of course." Brittany mounted Sugar Cookie in an easy motion and galloped beside him as he sped toward the mansion.

When they reached the stables, he jumped from Lightning's back and then looked over his shoulder at Brittany. She slid from Sugar Cookie's saddle then rubbed the mare's neck. Jerry jogged over and took the horses. Daniel knew his groom would take care of cooling them down, so he didn't bother issuing the order. He had a more important matter to attend to.

He strode down the path, over the brick patio and into the house, not stopping until he reached the living room where Emma was pacing. A large red-plaid suitcase leaned against the sofa. When Emma heard his footsteps on the hardwood floor, she turned to look at him. Even through his worry and anger, he recognized the grief in her eyes.

"Where do you think you're going?" he demanded. "We have a contract. Remember? One that I fully intend to enforce."

"I'm sorry, Mr. Dubois, but my father had a heart attack. I have to go home today. Now. I have to leave right now."

Daniel ran a frustrated hand over his face. He knew it was irrational to demand that she stay given the circumstances. He'd lost his parents three years ago, barely five months apart. They'd married when they were both twenty-one and Daniel's father hadn't been able to live without the love of his life. Though Daniel's mother had succumbed to breast cancer, his father had died of a broken heart.

Despite knowing how he should behave, Daniel struggled to find the compassion inside himself.

"I'm sorry, Mr. Dubois. You can sue me for everything I have, if that's what you want to do. But my father needs me and I'm going to be there for him."

As Daniel and Emma faced off, he became aware that Brittany was staring at the two of them in confusion. Clearly, she was trying to make sense of the conversation. Not that any of this was her business. His private life was his own, a concept he would obviously need to reinforce once—*if*—they began working together.

"Then go." What else could he say? He couldn't imprison her. If she wanted to leave, she would.

Emma grabbed her suitcase and darted from the room without looking back.

A cry cut through the tense silence. Without a word to Brittany, Daniel sprinted from the room and up the stairs to the nursery. Hailey was sitting, gnawing on a rail of her crib. When she saw him, she wiggled on her bottom and gave him a four-tooth grin Smiling, he picked her up and held her warm body against his chest.

He really loved his little girl. Why was it so hard to get the day-to-day right?

Hailey babbled something to him in a language only she understood. When he didn't respond, she slapped her hand against his cheek as if demanding he snap out of it. Right. She needed a new diaper. She might be chatting happily right now, but experience had taught him that if he didn't get her into a dry diaper soon, she'd be howling like a wolf.

Carrying her to the changing table, he laid her down and put a hand on her stomach, holding her in place. She gurgled and wiggled her chubby little body. He grabbed a wipe and a diaper and expertly changed Hailey. Her clothes had gotten wet during her nap, so he swiftly changed those, as well. Then he took her back downstairs for a snack.

He was on his way to the kitchen when he remembered that Brittany was still there. Making a U-turn, he went back to the front room.

Brittany, who'd been staring out the window, looked around as he stepped into the room. Her eyes widened in surprise when she saw the baby, but she merely smiled.

"Who have we here?" Brittany said,

"This is Hailey."

Brittany's her mouth dropped open, her full lips forming a perfect "O". She blinked then regained her composure. "I see." She leaned closer to look straight at the baby. "Hello, cutie pie."

Hailey chattered a greeting and then reached out her arms to Brittany.

That was different. Hailey generally didn't take to strangers. That's why he'd tried so hard to hold on to Emma. She and Hailey had bonded. Before Emma, Hailey had spent most of the day crying. After Emma, Hailey had gradually become happy. She'd even begun going down for naps without a fight and Daniel had been able to get some work done. He would have his work cut out for him until he found another nanny.

Emma's quitting couldn't have come at a worse time. Still, he'd adapt the same as he had when Hailey had unexpectedly come into his life.

Brittany touched Hailey's dimpled finger then looked at him. "I didn't know you were married."

"I'm not."

"Okay…"

This wasn't going well. Brittany was clearly confused and slightly put out, not that he blamed her. There had been some low-key flirting between them and now he was standing there with a baby in his arms. Although there wasn't anything between them—and given that his life was in a shambles and he wouldn't be involved with her or anyone else in the future—he didn't want her to get the wrong impression of him. His reputation meant everything to him. But he couldn't worry about her feelings or her opinion of him now. He had to take care of Hailey, who was squirming in his arms. He set her down and she immediately giggled.

"We're going to have to end our meeting now. Obviously. Since I no longer have a nanny, I have to take care of the baby. We'll have to reschedule."

"That's not necessary. I have enough information to get started."

"You do?"

"Yes. I'll work up a few options and get back to you in a few days with my suggestions."

Hailey crawled over to Brittany and yanked on her pant leg. Daniel reached down to grab Hailey at the same time Brittany bent and scooped her up. Immediately, Hailey grabbed Brittany's hair and gave it a hard tug. Without missing a beat, Brittany pulled her curls from the baby's hand.

He took Hailey into his arms again.

"It looks like you're going to need a new nanny. I can ask around if you want."

"Absolutely not." His voice was louder than he'd intended and Brittany jumped. He didn't apologize, though. He needed to make himself perfectly clear. "You are not to tell anyone about Hailey, is that clear? Your job depends on it. If you breathe one word to anyone about Hailey's existence, I'll make your life a living hell."

She slammed her hands on her hips. "There's no need to be nasty. And threats don't work with me. All you had to do was ask me to keep your secret and I would have agreed. Gossiping about you is the last thing I plan on doing."

"Fine."

"Fine."

They stared at one another, each breathing hard and neither speaking. He had to give it to her. She wasn't one to back down.

Hailey let out a whimper, ending the senseless standoff. Brittany stalked into his office then returned with her satchel and purse.

"You've got your hands full, literally and figuratively, so I'll leave. I'll contact you when I have something to share so we can discuss our next steps."

"You're assuming you have the job. I haven't seen your plans yet. I might not like them."

She frowned. "Fair enough. I'll work up preliminary plans and get them to you. Then you can decide what you want to do next."

Daniel walked her to the door and watched as she made her way to her car. When he caught himself admiring the gentle sway of her hips, he shut the door. There wasn't even enough space in his life for the no-strings relationships he preferred. Not that it mattered. Brittany was going to be working for him, setting her on the other side of a line he would never cross. Business and personal were never allowed to mingle. Too bad, he thought as he returned to the living room, the baby in his arms. Too, too bad. Because this was one time he wouldn't be opposed to them mixing.

Chapter Three

Brittany felt Daniel's eyes on her as she walked to her car. That had to have been the most bizarre meeting she'd ever had. And she'd had some doozies in her time. She'd been challenged, flirted with, insulted and threatened all in the space of a few hours. Flustering her was difficult, but he'd come close to knocking her off her game.

Daniel's reputation as a hard-nosed businessman was well established throughout Bronco, although, other than that he was single, very little was known about his personal life. But not from lack of trying. She'd scoured the internet for information about him to prepare for this meeting. Apart from the pictures of him with various women at public functions and the information provided by his company, there was nothing about his private life. Certainly there had been no hint of a baby.

The busybodies in town had worked over-time trying to dig up tidbits about the man's personal life. She had no intention of shar-ing what she'd learned with them. Or anyone.

Not that she was afraid of him or his threats. She wasn't. But she wasn't a gossip, either. Though she'd never been the victim of wag-ging tongues, she knew the harm that could result from loose talk. And, really, was the fact that he had a baby anyone's business? Still, the fact that he was a father had come as a shock.

As she drove back to her office, she forced all thoughts of Daniel's status as a parent from her mind and began to work out plans for his event. The ideas were coming fast and furi-ous, but since she was driving, she couldn't write them down. So she began to sing them aloud. Long ago she'd discovered that creating lyrics for important information and singing them over and over helped her remember. That's how she'd helped her youngest sister pass eighth-grade science. Even now they still laughed at the esophagus-liver-stomach song whenever they got together.

Singing to herself about color schemes and centerpieces, she parked and went to her office where she booted up her computer then furiously typed her ideas for the party. Once that was done, she printed out a copy to take home to review later then turned off her computer.

It was the end of the workday and she could hear her coworkers bustling about as they prepared to leave. There was a knock on her door. Before Brittany could say a word, Julia, another event planner and one of Brittany's closest friends, opened the door and poked her head inside. "We're going out for drinks at BB&G. You want to come?"

Brittany often joined her friends for drinks

and dinner after work, but today she turned them down. There was so much she needed to do for Daniel's event. Besides, she was distracted with thoughts of him and knew if she was questioned about it, she would probably blurt out something she shouldn't.

"Not tonight. It's been a busy day and I think I'll just go on home. You guys have fun."

"We'll miss you. See you tomorrow."

"Bye." Brittany grabbed her purse and satchel and headed out of the office, to the building's private parking lot and her car. In a few minutes she'd left downtown behind and was on her way to Bronco Heights and the condo she shared with her roommate, Amanda Jenkins.

Amanda was home when Brittany arrived, which was a pleasant surprise. Now that Amanda was engaged, she spent a lot of time with her fiancé, Holt Dalton. Even though Brittany didn't want to get married, she wasn't opposed to the institution. She was happy that her shy friend had found the love of her life.

"Hey," Brittany said, slipping off her shoes.

"Hi." Amanda looked up from the bridal magazine she was skimming, a smile on her face. She brushed her long brown hair over her shoulder.

A pile of other bridal magazines sat on Brittany's favorite chair, so she gathered them up and set them on the coffee table before sitting down. "How goes the dress hunt?"

"Oh, I'm still just getting ideas. I'm trying to figure out what I like and what I wouldn't be caught dead in."

Brittany laughed. Amanda was petite and quite pretty, something she didn't seem to know. "You're gorgeous and have a great figure. You'll look great in any style. You'd just better not make us bridesmaids wear some strange, never-worn-anywhere-in-the-real-world-created-by-a-design-school-dropout dress."

"Not to worry. You'll be able to pick your own dress."

"Really? Thank goodness. I have a closet full of horrible bridesmaids' dresses that I will never wear. Those things are so ugly, I can't even give them away."

Amanda set aside the magazine. "Enough about the wedding. How was your meeting with Daniel Dubois?"

Brittany curled her feet underneath her. "Interesting."

"Come on. That tells me exactly nothing."

"He wasn't what I expected. And at the same time, he's exactly what I expected."

Amanda laughed. "Mud would be clearer."

"I guess that didn't make sense. Here's the thing. Everybody knows that Daniel Dubois is a hard-nosed businessman. He demands to have things his way. And because he's extremely rich, people usually give in to him."

"Sounds about right."

"But there's more to him than that. When we were riding horses, he was friendly. Funny. Charming." He'd looked so rugged and handsome sitting on that magnificent stallion—like an ad for outdoor living at its finest. He would be the perfect model for any brochures advertising his dude ranch. Of course, she knew without asking that he'd never agree to such a thing. That was too bad. Beauty like his should be shared with the masses.

Amanda made the timeout signal with her hands. "Hold on. When were the two of you riding horses? I thought you had a business meeting."

"We did. Afterward he wanted to show me his property. He owns a horse ranch, and I ride, so it only made sense to see his place on horseback."

"Really? That sounds like a date to me."

"It wasn't. It was business."

"So you say. But why did you need to see his ranch? It's certainly isn't necessary in order to organize his party."

"Who am I to question him? He's the client. He wanted to show me the ranch, so I went." And she'd enjoyed herself immensely. Those quiet moments they'd shared admiring the beauty of the waterfall far surpassed any of her recent dates.

"Mmm-hmm."

"What does that mean?"

"It means that you went from really disliking that man and only working with him as a means to an end, to describing him as charming. Your interest in him sounds more than professional."

"Being in love has addled your brain. You're seeing love and romance when there isn't any."

Amanda's brown eyes sparkled with amusement. "Oh ho, who said anything about love or romance? I just said that you're interested in him."

"I'm not." Brittany was definite about that. Sure, the man had an undeniable magnetism. What woman wouldn't feel a tug on everything that was feminine in his presence? But that perfectly human reaction didn't alter her life plans. The only thing she wanted from Daniel Dubois was his business. She wasn't interested in becoming involved with him— or any man for that matter.

Not that she didn't date. She did. But much

to her parents' dismay, she wasn't looking for a serious relationship. A husband and kids were the furthest thing from her mind. Perhaps her lack of interest stemmed from the memories of caring for her siblings. Or maybe it came from seeing how exhausted her mother had been. Her mother had worked almost as many hours at the cleaners as Brittany's father had. Then she'd come home and take care of her kids. She'd never had a minute to herself.

Brittany was determined to take a different path, which was why marriage wasn't on her agenda. And kids were out of the question. Other thirty-three-year-old women might hear a ticking biological clock, but not her. She didn't hear a thing. In fact, her clock might not even be plugged in.

Her mother insisted that when she met *the one*, whoever that mythical man might be, she'd be ready to settle down and have babies. Not likely. Brittany had big plans that didn't include becoming Mrs. Anybody and raising kids. Besides, Daniel's life was complicated. He had an infant. Even if Brittany was willing to consider a relationship with him—which she wasn't—his daughter was a deal breaker. Brittany liked kids, but she didn't want any of her own. She'd seen the toll being a working mother had taken on her mother. Mallory Brandt had been exhausted most of Brittany's life. And since Brittany had no plans to give up her career, kids were out.

She wasn't cut out to be a mother with the full-time responsibility that came along with having kids. That wasn't the life for her. She'd be the favorite aunt to her siblings' and friends' kids, taking them on fun outings, letting them have sleepovers at her house, and buying them ridiculously expensive gifts, but that was it.

Despite all the reasons he was wrong for her, there was something about Daniel that had reached out to her on an elemental level. Though she might not want to admit it, something in her had reached back.

"Deny all you want, if that makes you

happy. But remember, when you and Daniel do get together, I reserve the right to say I told you so. Oh, and I expect all of the details."

Brittany laughed as she stood. "You'll be the first to know. On that note, I'm going to say good-night and leave you to your dress hunt. See you in the morning."

After heating up leftover meatloaf she'd brought home from dinner with her parents earlier in the week, Brittany went into her room. She loved the condo she and Amanda shared, but her bedroom suite was her sanctuary. She'd decorated it in soothing creams, whites and pale blues. Personal pictures were scattered across her dresser and bedside tables. Her desk was situated beneath the windows, where she was able to enjoy a view of nature whenever she worked there.

She took out her notes with the intention of adding contacts so she could hit the ground running tomorrow morning. She'd pull out all the stops and call in every favor she'd earned to make this dinner the talk of the town.

But rather than work, she sat there, pen in

hand and stared out her window. Instead of her normal view of trees, a manicured lawn, with perfectly spaced flowers, she saw Daniel astride his magnificent horse, galloping across the untouched beauty of his ranch. To her. When he reached her, he jumped from his stallion and closed the distance between them. Smiling, he held out a hand to touch her face. Then he lowered his head as she raised hers to receive his kiss. Just as their lips were about to meet, an owl hooted, and Brittany jerked. Blinking, she tried to clear her head.

What in the world was she doing? Why was she daydreaming about Daniel? He was her client. And he had a child. Either one of those things alone should have given her pause. Both together should have made her stop and then run in the other direction. The fact that she was fantasizing about him scared her witless.

"I'm coming," Daniel said more to himself than to Hailey. For the past few days, he'd been caring for the baby on his own as well as trying to get his business up and running. Caring for Hailey took priority, so he generally didn't get much work done during the day. By the time she was asleep at night, he was all but worn out. In the past, he'd put in long hours, rising with the sun and working well into the night without a problem. But in those days, he hadn't been caring for a child.

Who knew someone so small could be so draining?

Hailey was screaming at the top of her lungs by the time he reached the nursery. It was only four in the morning and, hoping she'd fall back to sleep, he didn't turn on the light. A quick check revealed that her diaper was still dry, so that wasn't the source of her displeasure. Holding her against his chest, he sat in the glider and began to rock back and forth. Though she was no longer screeching, Hailey still cried. She didn't feel warm, so he had no clue about what was wrong.

"Did you have a nightmare?" he asked, rubbing his hand up and down her back in a soothing motion. "Or are you missing your mommy?"

Daniel knew he did. He still couldn't believe Jane was gone. If only he could go back in time and change things, he would. Instead he was forced to live with the reality that the past couldn't be altered. He wanted Hailey to know about her mother. And when she was older, he would tell her. At least he'd tell her the positive things he remembered about his sweet little sister. After all, he wanted Hailey to have a positive image of her mother.

Daniel would have liked to tell her about her father, too, but other than the man's name—Craig Larimar—Daniel didn't know anything. He'd never met the man who'd fathered his sister's child. And since he'd died in the same accident that had claimed Jane, Daniel never would. He'd have to be satisfied with telling Hailey that her father had loved her.

"Your mother would be so proud of you," he said to Hailey, whose sobs had finally stopped. "She loved you very much. She wanted me to raise you as my own child and that's what I'm going to do. I love you, too. Very much."

"Badanappa."

"Why, yes, it would be nice if you would go back to sleep."

She laughed and clapped her hands.

He laughed softly. "I hope that means you agree with my suggestion."

"Batba ooh ooh."

Daniel didn't reply, not wanting to prolong the conversation. Instead he rocked slowly until Hailey fell back to sleep. Rising carefully, he put her into her crib and covered her with the light blanket. With any luck, she would sleep for the rest of the night.

One thing was certain. He couldn't go on like this much longer. He needed help. Perhaps he should have taken Brittany up on her offer to help him find a new nanny. But that would mean letting the people in Bronco learn about Hailey. So far, he'd been able to keep her existence a secret and wanted to keep it that way.

He'd learned at a young age to guard his

private life. Although he'd prefer not to be mentioned in the press, it had been part and parcel of starting a successful company in his twenties. He'd had to do interviews and make himself available to be photographed. But even then, he'd avoided answering questions about his family and personal life.

Protecting his privacy had been important before, but it was essential now that he had Hailey. She deserved to have as normal a childhood as he could give her. Being followed by press and having her picture splashed all over the internet so people he didn't know and who didn't know them could get a glimpse of her made his stomach twist in knots. Still, he had to do something.

He kissed her soft cheek. "Sleep well, little one."

Daniel didn't return to his room, going instead to his office. There would be no more sleep for him tonight, so he may as well get some work done. Hopefully, he'd hear from Brittany soon with her ideas for the party.

He really was looking forward to talking to her, and not just about her ideas. She was an attractive woman with a lot of spunk. Under other circumstances, he might have pursued her.

Sadly, these weren't other circumstances. And if he liked her proposal, she would be working for him. Their relationship needed to remain strictly professional.

Now he just had to figure out a way to keep her from invading his thoughts night and day.

Chapter Four

Brittany took the last paper from the printer, stacked all of the pages neatly, then inserted them into a folder. She'd outdone herself and was pleased with the results. Every vendor she'd sought out had been available and had given her reasonable quotes. She never liked to skimp on cost, believing you ultimately paid if you tried to nickel-and-dime people, but she didn't like to overpay, either, no matter how wealthy her client. She preferred to have win-win deals. That way, vendors would want to work with her again as well as accommodate special requests.

She hadn't heard from Daniel in the past few days, which gave her pause. She'd left two messages for him, but he hadn't responded. As far as she knew, he hadn't hired another firm and she was still working for him, so she needed to update him on her plans and get his go-ahead to proceed. If he wanted to make changes, now was the time.

Since he also wanted this event to occur as soon as possible, she needed his approval now. Leaving messages had been futile, so she had to try a different tact. She'd drop by his house. Stopping by without an appointment was a gamble, but it was a risk she was willing to take. If he wasn't available, she'd leave a copy of her plans with a member of his staff.

After letting Rachel know she'd be out of the office for a few hours, Brittany drove to the Dubois ranch. As before, she was struck by the beauty of his property. It was nature at its absolute most stunning. She could only dream of waking up to this beauty every morning; of walking through the grass to the lake every day. But since she was only here for business and not to move in, imagining was as close as she would get.

She parked in the driveway and headed to his front door. The closer she got to the house, the harder her heart began to thump. She inhaled deeply, trying to calm her suddenly jittery nerves. She didn't understand the reaction. She had follow-up meetings with clients all the time and never got nervous. In fact, meeting with clients generally energized her.

Blowing out the breath, she forced herself to admit the truth. Her blood wasn't racing through her veins because she was concerned about the meeting. She was reacting this way in anticipation of seeing Daniel again. Though she was loathe to admit it, she'd been thinking of him quite a bit these past few days. He'd invaded her thoughts at the most inopportune times, not that any time would be good. But no matter how many lectures she gave herself, she'd found herself daydreaming about him.

Well, that wouldn't do. He was her client and she had her rules. Straightening her shoulders, she rang the doorbell. Before it stopped ringing, the door swung open.

"Hello, Ms. Brandt."

"Hi, Marta," Brittany replied, grateful for the warm greeting. "I realize I've dropped by unannounced, but I'm wondering if Mr. Dubois is available to meet."

"I'll check. Come inside."

Brittany waited in the foyer for a minute or two. She was reconsidering the wisdom of her impulsive trip out here when Marta returned. "Mr. Dubois is available. Follow me, please."

Brittany expected to be shown into Daniel's office, but instead she was led deep into yet another wing of the house to an enormous family room. Daniel was sitting on a comfy-looking couch, Hailey on his lap. Whereas his clothes had been neat, if not immaculate when she'd last seen him, he now looked slightly disheveled. Orange specks of what was probably strained peaches dotted the front of his wrinkled shirt. He didn't seem to notice. Or maybe he was just past caring.

The look on his face gave away his exhaustion. His deep brown eyes were red-rimmed and puffy. And it looked like he hadn't shaved in a couple of days. He stifled a yawn, confirming what she'd already surmised. He needed rest.

He glanced at her ruefully, rubbing the stubble on his chin. "Sorry I haven't called you back. I intended to, but Hailey has been fussy lately and not in the mood to cooperate with me."

"I take it you haven't found a nanny yet."

"No." He heaved a deep sigh. "My staff have pitched in when they could, but Hailey hasn't warmed up to them. Besides, she's my responsibility, not theirs."

Brittany resisted the urge to repeat her offer to help him find another nanny. The last time she'd made the suggestion, he'd bitten off her head and threatened her. If he wanted her help, he was going to have to ask for it. Yet a piece of her heart ached for him. She remembered how worn out her mother had been when Brittany's siblings had been little. Babies might be adorable, but they were exhausting.

At the sound of Brittany's voice, Hailey turned and gave a bright smile, showing off her four teeth. She might be the cutest baby Brittany had ever seen, but she wasn't fooled. She knew Hailey would give her a run for her money in a minute.

"I stopped by to go over my proposal with you, but I can tell you're busy. I'll just leave a copy of it with you, so you can read it at your leisure."

"Leisure. That's a distant memory. Kind of like a good night's sleep. If you don't mind, I'd like to go over the proposal with you now."

Hailey rattled off a few nonsensical words then stretched out her arms in Brittany's direction.

Daniel covered another yawn. "I know I rejected your offer to help me find a nanny, but if it still stands, I'd like to take you up on it."

"Sure. I can ask around. I won't let anyone know it's for you. I'll just say a friend is looking for help. How's that?"

His bleary eyes widened in surprise. What? Did he think she didn't recall how he'd freaked out at the idea of anyone knowing about Hailey? She didn't know why he felt that way, but it wasn't her business. She could help him and allow him to maintain his privacy.

"That sounds perfect. Thank you. And let me take this time to apologize for being a jerk. I was a bit stressed the other day, but that's no excuse for how I treated you. I'm sorry."

Brittany hoped she covered her surprise better than he had. "You're forgiven."

"Thanks."

They shared a smile and Brittany's heart went pitter-patter. It was foolish and a bit dangerous to give her attraction to this man even a breath of air, but apparently she wasn't as smart as she'd liked to believe. Luckily, they weren't going to be in each other's lives for much longer. If he approved her proposal, she would set her plan into action and not see him again until a day or two before the dinner. Once the event was over, they would go back to their regularly scheduled lives. Since their social circles didn't overlap—he was a wealthy rancher and she was a middle-class working girl—it was unlikely their paths would cross again.

Mr. Rogers, Daniel's butler, entered the room. "Sorry to interrupt, but you have an important call from Dallas."

"I'm in the middle of a meeting," Daniel said. "Take a message and I'll call back."

"You'll want to take this call."

"Who is it?"

"A man with the last name of Larimar."

Daniel stiffened. "Right."

Brittany looked from Daniel to Mr. Rogers, who wore a somber expression.

"Would you mind watching Hailey for me while I take this call?" Daniel asked.

"Uh," Brittany uttered as words failed her. Daniel must have taken that sound as a yes because he stood and handed over Hailey, who immediately grabbed the front of Brittany's shirt in her tiny hands. For someone so small, Hailey had quite the grip.

Mr. Rogers followed Daniel from the room, leaving Brittany alone with the baby. Hailey blew spit bubbles and giggled at her accomplishment. After a moment, she pushed away and tried to slide down Brittany's body.

"I take it you want to get down," Brittany said, bending to set the baby on the floor. Hailey bounced her bottom on the thick rug centered on the dark hardwood. A few seconds later, she got on all fours and crawled with amazing speed across the floor. When she reached a leather ottoman in front of an oversize chair near the unlit fireplace, she tried to pull herself up. Brittany crossed the room and sat on the floor beside her. "Well, let's see what you can do."

Hailey stopped moving long enough to string together a bunch of syllables before returning to her chosen task. When she was standing, Hailey looked at Brittany, let go of the furniture and wobbled for a moment before plopping back down on her bottom.

Undaunted, she grabbed hold of the ottoman and began to climb again. Within seconds, she was on her feet. Chortling happily, she began bouncing up and down in what Brittany surmised was the baby version of the happy dance.

Brittany heard footsteps and placed a hand on the baby's back before turning around. Daniel was standing there. The color had drained from his face and he looked distraught. Shaken.

"Is everything okay?" Brittany asked.

He shook his head. "Look, I need a favor. I know this is an unusual request in a business meeting, but would you mind keeping an eye on Hailey for a while longer? I have no idea how long I'll be. I need to call my lawyer. I would ask one of my staff, but to be honest, she hasn't bonded with them the way she has with you. She cries when she's left with any of them. I'll pay you for your time, of course."

"Oh. Sure."

"I know this wasn't how you expected to spend your time and I appreciate your help."

"I'm a full-service event planner." Brittany smiled, but it wasn't returned.

"Thanks. I'll just be in my office. I'll be back as soon as I can."

Daniel was out of the room before Brittany could even nod.

"Intense. Your daddy is intense," Brittany said to Hailey.

"Bah," Hailey replied.

Brittany laughed. Although she hadn't planned on babysitting, spending time with Hailey was actually kind of fun. None of Brittany's siblings or close friends had infants, so she didn't spend much time with babies. Though she'd thought she'd gotten her fill of little ones when she'd been tasked with taking care of her siblings, she'd been wrong. Being with Hailey was a nice change of pace. Being responsible for Hailey wasn't something Brittany would choose to do every day, but today was novel and enjoyable.

Hailey let go of the ottoman, teetered on her feet then landed on her diapered bottom. Her lip quivered as if she was about to cry.

"Oh no you don't." Brittany scooped Hailey onto her lap then buried her face in her neck, kissing her sweet baby skin.

Hailey giggled, so Brittany did it again. Then she moved on to Hailey's chubby belly and planted kisses there, making Hailey laugh loud and long. They were still playing when Daniel returned. One look at the strained expression on his face and Brittany knew that the conversation with his lawyer hadn't gone the way he'd hoped.

Brittany stood, Hailey in her arms. "You don't look so good. Is there anything I can do to help?"

Daniel didn't say anything, but any number of emotions raced across his face, ranging from despair to hope before finally settling on determination.

"Actually, there is something you can do to help me."

"Name it."

"You can marry me."

"Say what now?"

"You can marry me," he said. Initially when

he'd blurted out the words, the idea was still forming in his mind and he'd been speaking out of desperation. But now that he'd said it, the idea was starting to take hold.

The first call he'd received had been from Craig Larimar's parents. Hailey's paternal grandparents. They'd only just learned that their son was dead and that their granddaughter was, in their words, living with a stranger in Montana. They demanded immediate custody of Hailey.

A few weeks ago, he might have been relieved that someone else wanted the responsibility of caring for Hailey. Back then, he would have been glad to be relegated to the role of doting uncle. He would have happily kept his bachelor lifestyle while making frequent visits to his niece. But that was then. This was now. It might not be official yet—something he intended to remedy immediately—but he loved Hailey as if she were his biological child. There was no way he would give her up without a fight. Besides, it was Jane's dying wish that he raise her child. He might have failed his sister in life, but there was no way he was going to fail her in death.

Unfortunately, since there was nothing in writing, his case wasn't as strong as he would have liked. As the Larimars astutely pointed out, they were a married couple while he was a bachelor with a reputation as a ladies' man.

Though his lawyer, John Kirkland, had told him there was a good chance he would prevail in court, that wasn't good enough. Even the slightest possibility of losing Hailey was too great a risk. He needed to improve the odds so there was no doubt that the judge would grant him custody. John had mentioned that it was too bad Daniel wasn't married, planting an idea in Daniel's mind.

If he was going to compete with a married couple, he needed to have a wife by his side to balance the scales. And not just any woman. He needed someone who would impress the judge. Someone with an impeccable character. Most importantly, he needed someone who'd bonded with Hailey. Someone who Hailey responded to. He'd thought it was a fluke that first day when Hailey had seemed to like Brittany enough to let her pick her up. But after seeing them playing right now, he knew that Brittany would be the perfect person to bring into their lives until the custody battle with the Larimars was resolved.

He needed Brittany to marry him.

Brittany reared back and a confused expression crossed her beautiful face. Then she laughed. "Good one. And clever. You say something outrageous so I'll be more inclined to agree to what you really want. So now that you've shocked me, why don't you tell me what you actually want?"

"I want you to marry me."

She shook her head, handed Hailey to him and took a step back. "I think I need to leave."

He stepped in front of her and put a hand on her arm. "Wait. Please. I'm not doing a good job of explaining. I'm still trying to figure it all out. Give me a minute, okay?"

"A minute to what? What do you think is going to change in a minute? Or ten minutes?"

"Your mind?"

She stepped around him.

If he had a chance of convincing her to agree, he had to tell her everything about Jane and Hailey. "Hailey isn't my daughter. She's my niece, and I'm about to be engaged in a custody battle."

"Say what?"

"Can we sit down and talk?"

She hesitated for the longest seconds of his life. "Fine."

He put an arm around her waist and guided her toward the sofa. When they reached it, she perched on the edge, as if poised to flee if he made one false move. He'd made a mess of things. Rather than lead with a proposal, he should have given her the backstory and gained her sympathy. Heck, if he'd said it right, she might have been the one to bring up marriage. Well, it was too late to start over. He'd just have to plow through.

Daniel settled Hailey into her baby saucer. Once she was contentedly swatting at a purple star that bounced up and down, Daniel turned back to Brittany. "It's a long story."

"I have time. And if you plan on convincing me, I suggest you don't leave anything out."

"I'll start at the beginning."

"That's always the best place."

She still sounded shocked, but given the circumstances, that was to be expected. And she hadn't left, which gave him hope that she'd actually listen to what he had to say, and his fear subsided.

"Like I said, Hailey is my niece. She was my younger sister's daughter. Jane was wonderful. So pretty." He paused, letting the past wash over him.

"I remember the day my mom and dad brought her home from the hospital. She was so tiny. Even though I was only five, I knew she was special. I promised to be the best big brother in the world.

"I adored Jane and she loved me, too. She liked to follow me around when we were kids." He'd included her as much as he could when he'd played with his friends.

He looked at Brittany. She was following his story intently.

"As I got older, I focused more on my studies. Actually, school was kind of easy for me. I skipped second and fifth grades. I earned my high school diploma in three years and started college at sixteen. But I went to school out east, so it was too far away for me to visit a lot. When I did come home for summer vacations, I worked construction and spent time with my friends, and it didn't leave me a lot of time for Jane. Because I'd been distracted by my life, I hadn't noticed the changes in hers."

But he should have. And he would have if he'd bothered to look.

"What kind of changes?"

"Jane had struggled with depression and an eating disorder. Bulimia. She'd always been what our mother had referred to as 'pleasingly plump.' Jane hadn't seen her body that way. Neither had the bullies in her high school, whose taunts only echoed the dark emotions that plagued her, feelings she'd been powerless to control.

"Our parents were big believers in higher education, and they'd wanted her to go to college. But she'd hated school and couldn't wait to be done. When she graduated from high school, she got a job as a waitress and moved out of our parents' house. After that, she barely kept in touch with them. Or me."

That had hurt. He and Jane had been so close as children. He'd recognized his own responsibility in letting the relationship fade when he went away to school, and tried to keep in touch with her, but she'd grown distant, too. She hadn't wanted him in her life in any significant way.

"It was obvious that she was floundering. Our parents tried everything they could to help her, offering to go with her to therapy, but all of their efforts failed. They just hadn't been able to reach her."

Daniel, too, had done his best to help Jane, offering to help with her bills or help her find a therapist she would trust, but nothing seemed to work. Time and distance had severed the bonds that once had seemed unbreakable.

Once their parents were gone, Jane hadn't seen the need to maintain even minimal contact with him. May God forgive him, Daniel hadn't forced the issue. He hadn't tried as hard as he should have to remain a part of Jane's life. Her repeated rejections had torn him apart. He'd loved her and thought eventually she'd recognize that and come back around.

"Then one day she was gone without a trace. I searched for her, but she'd vanished. It was as if she'd dropped off the face of the earth. When I couldn't find her, I hired a private investigator. She tracked her to a house in a Dallas suburb. At the time, I was still living in Texas while this house was being built. She didn't look good, so I asked her to move in with me. Not for forever. Just long enough for her to get well. She said no."

He hadn't been trying to run her life as Jane had accused. All he'd wanted to do was help her get healthy. She'd been so distant.

So aloof. It was as if she was no longer the little sister he'd adored. No, that sweet young woman had been replaced by a stranger. She'd claimed she needed to stay where she was. She hadn't elaborated. Nor had she mentioned being pregnant.

"I tried to keep in touch, asking her to meet for lunch or dinner or just to talk on the phone, but Jane kept rejecting me. One day I showed up at her house only to discover that she'd moved out. She hadn't left a forwarding address. And she'd changed her cell phone number. She was gone."

He looked at Brittany and saw the sympathy in her eyes. He'd never revealed just how devastating Jane's rejection had been. He hadn't said the words, but he knew Brittany understood.

He tried to tell the story unemotionally, but his voice cracked on the last word. He cleared his throat and soldiered on. "I could have tracked her down again, but I didn't. What would have been the point? I decided to give her space, since that was apparently what she wanted. That was a horrible mistake." One he'd yet to get over.

"The next time I heard Jane's name was a little over a month ago from a police detective. She was dead."

"Oh, Daniel. I'm so sorry."

So was he. But that didn't change a thing. The little sister he'd adored was gone. He'd failed her and now he'd never get a chance to make it up to her.

While grief and sorrow had pounded Daniel's heart like a fist, the officer had continued talking. Jane had had a daughter. Daniel was her next of kin. Would he be willing to take care of his niece?

"That's when I found out about Hailey. Jane and the baby's father, Craig Larimar, had been in a car accident. Hailey had been strapped in her car seat, so she hadn't been harmed at all. Craig died at the scene. Jane…" He swallowed "They rushed Jane to the hospital, where she survived for a few hours. While she was there, she gave one of the nurses my name and told the nurse that she wanted me to raise Hailey."

Heartbroken over the loss of his sister, and grateful to have her child in his life, he'd brought Hailey home with him that day.

"Despite all my money, I couldn't help Jane. I couldn't make things better for her. Couldn't protect her from the world. I may have failed my sister, but I won't fail her child."

Brittany placed her hand over his. The warmth from her skin soothed some of the hurt in deep places he hadn't had a hope would ever stop aching.

"Looks to me like you're doing a great job. Hailey is happy and loved."

"That might not be enough now."

"Why not?"

"The phone call I just received was from Craig Larimar's parents. Apparently, they plan to sue me for custody of Hailey."

"I don't see what the problem is. Your sister wanted you to raise Hailey. Therefore you should win the case easily."

"I have no written proof of that. She didn't

have a will. And she'd never even mentioned me to any of her friends. Not only that, they're a couple. I'm a single man. And before I had Hailey to think about, I lived like a single man. I dated. A lot."

"So? That doesn't make you a bad person."

"But it doesn't make me father material, either."

"Says who? Single men can be great dads."

"I'll have a better chance of winning if I have a wife. Then it will be one married couple versus another. And we're younger, so that should give us the advantage."

"We?"

"Yes. We." He infused his voice with more confidence than he felt.

"I didn't agree to marry you." Her voice quivered, but he didn't know her well enough to tell if it was from nerves or irritation. Neither was welcome.

He tapped the tips of his fingers together, trying to cover his concern. Desperation was growing within him, but he didn't want her to see his weakness. This argument wasn't working. He needed to find a different way to convince her.

"What do you want, Brittany?"

"What do you mean what do I want?"

"I want to raise Hailey. Not just to honor my sister's wishes, but because I love her." He paused. "You're smart. Ambitious. Too smart and ambitious to work for someone else for the rest of your life."

"So?" She sounded cautious, but she hadn't gotten up and left.

"You'll want to open your own event planning business one day. I can help you do that. If you marry me, I'll give you all the money you need to start your business. Not only that, I'll introduce you to my friends and business associates, and suggest that they hire you to plan their events. With my help, your business will become a nationally recognized event planning company in no time."

"And all I have to do is marry you."

The flat tone of her voice worried him, but still he nodded. "Yes."

She slowly rose and straightened her shoulders, standing as erect as a queen. Luscious lips pinched and eyes narrowed, she glared at him. "I'm not for sale. Not to you or to anyone. I can't speak for Bronco Elite, but as for me, I will no longer be working on your party." She picked up the folder she'd brought him. "And you, Daniel Dubois, can go straight to hell."

"Wait." He reached for her to try to explain, but she brushed by him and out of the room. He hadn't meant to offend her. He'd only wanted to show her how marrying him could benefit both of them. Usually he was so much more eloquent than this. The fear of losing Hailey had turned him into a bumbling idiot.

Sagging back onto the couch, he decided that it was best to retreat and regroup. He'd shocked her. That was clear now. Given time, she would see the benefit of the deal he was offering and come around. A marriage between them would be a win-win situation.

Now he just had to come up with a plan to convince her.

Chapter Five

Brittany stormed down the walk, jumped into her car and sped down the driveway. Inhaling deeply, she tried to center herself, but she couldn't. She was too furious. Had that man really tried to buy her like a piece of meat? She wanted to own her own company, but selling herself wasn't part of the plan. She'd go back to working for that money-hungry Evan Cruise and that ghost tours company first. She couldn't believe Daniel Dubois thought so poorly of her that he believed she would sell herself. True, they'd only known each other for a short time, so he didn't know her character, but she'd thought he'd respected her as a person. Boy, had she been wrong.

As Brittany neared her office, she began to calm down. The conversation with Daniel, though insulting, was now in the past. Since she'd let him know in no uncertain terms that she was not for sale, she didn't expect to repeat the conversation anytime soon. But as she stepped into the building, worry began to gnaw at her insides.

Daniel Dubois was a powerful man who clearly thought he was entitled to whatever he believed his money could buy. What if he'd called her boss to complain? What if he'd insisted that she be fired, thinking that putting financial pressure on her might force her to give in to his demand? She wouldn't have suspected him of being that low before, but now? Now, she wouldn't put anything past him.

Stepping inside the office, she looked around. Linnea, her boss, smiled as she came toward Brittany. "How did your meeting go?"

Brittany wasn't sure how to answer that. Mentioning that she'd told a client to go to hell didn't seem the way to go if she wanted to advance her career. Even if Linnea was willing to listen to Brittany's explanation, what could she say? That Daniel wanted to marry her so he'd have a better chance of keeping custody of his niece? That might convince Linnea not to fire her, but Brittany knew Daniel didn't want anyone to know about Hailey. Even as hurt and angry—and yes, disappointed—as she was, she wouldn't betray his confidence. She had integrity even if he didn't.

Brittany opened her mouth to answer Linnea's question as honestly as possible when Reese, another one of the event planners, approached. "Sorry to interrupt. Linnea, do you have a minute?"

Linnea looked at Brittany, who nodded. "We can catch up later. I don't have anything new to tell you at this point."

"Good enough," Linnea said as she and Reese walked away.

Brittany sighed with relief as she went to

her office and closed the door. She didn't know how such a perfectly planned day had gone awry, but it had. Now she had to figure out how to get the proverbial train back on the tracks.

She managed to keep her mind focused on work for the rest of the day. Since she hadn't been summoned to her boss's office and read the riot act, she surmised that Daniel hadn't called to complain. And since she didn't want to mention to her boss that she'd told a client to go to hell, there was no way around it. She was going to have to plan the event. That meant she was going to have to meet with him again. They hadn't discussed the details of the party today and she still needed him to sign off on her ideas and menu suggestions.

Given his home situation, she didn't expect him to come to her office. She doubted he'd be leaving his ranch in the next few days. So she had no choice but to meet with him at his house again. Fine. She was a professional. She could handle that. She'd do whatever was necessary to get this project over and done with as soon as possible so she wouldn't have to see him again.

But she wouldn't mind seeing that cutie pie Hailey again. Not that she was becoming attached to that sweet baby. She wasn't. Brittany had just enjoyed spending time with her, that was all.

Amanda wasn't home when Brittany got there, so she decided to make an early night of it. After soaking in the tub long enough for her fingers to prune, she smoothed on lotion, put on her favorite silk pajamas, wrapped her hair and then got into bed. Closing her eyes, Brittany instantly fell asleep. But instead of her normal peaceful rest, she dreamed she was alone in her apartment. There was a baby crying, but no matter where Brittany looked, she couldn't find the baby. The crying grew louder and more despondent, and Brittany became more frantic in her futile search. She called out to the baby that she was coming, but she never did find the child and the crying never stopped.

Brittany awoke with a jerk, tangled in her

sheets. Sitting up, she wiped a palm across her sweaty forehead. She leaned against the headboard and then checked the clock on her bedside table. Four thirty. Way too early to get up, yet she didn't think she'd be able to fall asleep again. She wasn't sure she wanted to. She might not be a psychiatrist, but even she could interpret this dream. She was worried about Hailey. What would happen to her if she was taken from Daniel and placed with her grandparents? Would the older couple love her the way Daniel obviously did? Would all of the upheaval at such a young age affect her ability to bond with people in the future?

Brittany frowned. Why was she so worried about it? This wasn't her problem. She'd only just met Daniel and Hailey. Besides, Daniel had money and could afford the best lawyers. He could solve this problem without her help.

Brittany grabbed the mystery she'd been reading, determined to distract herself from a problem that wasn't hers. When, after finishing a few chapters, she still was on edge, she rose and took extra care getting ready for work. She wouldn't be able to function until she had clarified her status with Daniel. If they were going to move ahead with the party, she needed his approval. If not, she needed to know that, too.

She decided to stop by his ranch before going to the office to leave the information with Marta or Mr. Rogers.

Pulling into the driveway, she thought of one of her favorite movies, *Groundhog Day,* where the main character kept living the same day over and over. This wasn't quite the same, but she was spending quite a bit of time at the Dubois ranch trying to get Daniel to look at her work. Maybe today he actually would.

When the front door swung open, she was once again greeted by his smiling housekeeper. Despite Brittany's protests, Marta insisted on ushering her inside, through a different wing than she'd used before, and into an enormous kitchen. There were oceans of marble countertops, professional-grade appliances and cabinets that reached the high ceiling. The feature she liked the most was the wall of glass doors with its gorgeous view of nature. If she'd had even the slightest interest in cooking, this would be her dream kitchen.

Daniel was seated at the table, feeding Hailey, who was sitting in her high chair. The remains of a smashed banana and baby cereal were smeared in a plastic bowl. Bits of food were in Hailey's hair and on her face and scattered on the stone floor.

Daniel was so focused on getting Hailey to eat that he hadn't noticed Brittany enter the room, so she took a moment to study him. His broad shoulders moved beneath his shirt as he lifted the spoon to Hailey's mouth. The baby turned her head away from him and spotted Brittany. She babbled a few excited syllables while reaching out to Brittany.

Daniel turned his head and, when he saw Brittany, jumped to his feet. He brushed a hand over his shirt then flicked a gray lump of dried baby food onto the table. "I didn't think I would see you again."

He didn't sound particularly aggravated.

Actually he sounded relieved, which made her heartrate slow down.

"We never did discuss my ideas for the party. So, if you still want to work with my firm, I'm hoping you have time now."

"Of course I want to work with your firm, and you specifically. If I made you believe otherwise, I apologize. I really want to hear your ideas." He looked over at Hailey, who'd eaten all the breakfast she intended to eat and was straining against the belt securing her in the chair.

"I guess I should have called first."

"It wouldn't have made a difference. As you can see, we're already awake."

Brittany nodded. She knew from experience that there was no such thing as sleeping late with a baby in the house.

"And since my nanny search is going nowhere, I'm pretty much held captive in this house." He blew out a breath. "I have a few more agencies to call, but I'm not holding out hope. Until I find the right nanny, I'll be taking care of Hailey on my own." He removed the bowl from the tray and started to take Hailey from the high chair.

"You might want to wipe off her hands and face first. It'll save your clothes. And walls."

"Thanks. I should have thought of that." He dampened a dish towel and then cleaned the food from Hailey's hands and face. She protested a bit but didn't cry. When he was finished, he freed the baby and held her against his chest. "Let's go to the family room. She has toys there and we can go over everything."

Once Hailey was settled on the play mat, surrounded by toys, Daniel and Brittany sat on the couch. Brittany reached for her satchel, but Daniel put a hand on her wrist, stopping her. Electricity shot out from where their skin connected and raced through her body. *Darn it. Why was this still happening?*

"Before we start, I want to apologize to you. Again. I realize now how offensive my proposal must have sounded. I wasn't as eloquent as I would have liked to have been."

"Forget about it. I have." That wasn't exactly true. She'd thought about his crazy proposal more than she should have. In fact, it was all she could think of. But he didn't need to know that.

"I can't. I still think that having a wife will be the equalizer I need in the custody case. I'm a single man. It's no secret that I'm busy. Even though I work from home, I still put in long hours. A wife will help me prove that I can give Hailey a stable home."

"And you think a quickie marriage to your event planner will give you some sort of advantage?"

"I know you think it sounds outrageous, but hear me out." He leaned forward, his elbows on his knees. His voice was intent yet earnest. "We can make it work. I've seen you in action. You can easily accomplish anything you set your mind to. I believe you can play the role of wife and mother well enough to convince any social worker or judge that Hailey belongs here with me."

Brittany laughed. "I'm not some Mary Poppins or Suzie Homemaker. In case you haven't noticed, I'm not exactly maternal. I'm focused on my career. You were right. I do want to own my own business. All the social worker will have to do is ask a few people about me and your plan will crumble."

"So, you'll be a working mother. That's not so unusual."

She sputtered. "And I'm not much of a cook."

"You don't need to be. In case you haven't noticed, I employ a cook. And a housekeeper. All I need is for someone to play the role of wife and mother for the judge. I can take care of the rest."

She cleared her throat. "That's all?"

"What else would there be?"

She simply looked at him.

After a moment, his eyes narrowed as he understood her meaning. "I don't need to pay for female companionship. Not to be arrogant, but I have women throwing themselves at me all the time. I don't have to coerce a woman to get her into my bed."

Brittany fought off the twinge of something

that felt suspiciously like jealousy at the idea of another woman being in Daniel's bed. She brushed the idiotic thought aside. "Well, if you're so popular with the ladies, why don't you simply catch one of the ones throwing themselves at you?"

His mouth compressed as if he was suppressing a grin. When he spoke, there wasn't the least bit of mirth in his tone, so maybe she'd imagined the reaction. "Because Hailey has already bonded with you. That's rare for her. I won't be able to convince the judge that Hailey and my new wife have a loving mother/daughter relationship if Hailey fusses every time my wife comes within six feet of her. You might not think you're the maternal type, but you do a good imitation. I'm convinced that you care about Hailey enough to fool the judge or social worker.

"As I said a minute ago, ours would be a marriage of convenience. I'm willing to put that in writing, if that will make you feel better about our arrangement. Once a judge grants me full custody of Hailey, we can get an annulment. Then I'll give you any amount of money you want to finance your company. And I'll recommend you far and wide. I can have my attorney draw up everything. Or you can hire your own lawyer to represent your interests."

Her interests. He made it sound cut and dried—like a simple business deal. And to him, it was. But marriage was so much more than a business arrangement to advance one's cause, no matter how noble that cause might be. Her parents had been married for thirty-five years. Though Brittany had never liked the distribution of duties—she thought her mother did more than her share of the house-work and caring for the kids—she never once doubted her parents' devotion to one another. Her biological clock might not be ticking now, but she did want to get married one day and have the kind of marriage her parents had. Minus the kids.

"I'm sorry, Daniel. I just can't say yes. I hope my decision doesn't interfere with our working relationship. I know I can help you get your resort off to a great start."

He seemed to deflate with every word she spoke. Still, he didn't press her. "I'm sure you can."

She was under no obligation to marry him—in fact, she'd been clear from the beginning that she wouldn't. So why did guilt prick her conscience as if she'd done something wrong?

His cell phone rang. He checked the Caller ID and glanced at her. "Excuse me. I need to take this call."

"Of course."

Brittany didn't want to eavesdrop, so she went over to where Hailey was playing with brightly colored stackable plastic doughnuts and sat. Brittany's younger brothers had also had this toy and had played with it for hours on end. Hailey was chewing on the orange ring. She pulled the plastic from her mouth and, grinning, offered it to Brittany.

"No thanks. I only eat the yellow ones."

Hailey chortled as if she understood Brittany's joke.

Though she tried not to listen, she could hear Daniel's conversation. It was clear from his words that he wasn't succeeding in finding a nanny for Hailey. Would that hurt him in the custody case? If so, what would happen to the little tyke?

Finally, he ended the call and she returned to her seat.

"I guess you heard all that."

"Yes. I couldn't help but overhear."

"You must think I'm a manipulative jerk, but I'm not. I'm just desperate. Jane wanted me to raise Hailey. I have to fight for her. And win. That means that no tactic is off the table. I failed my sister when she was alive. I should have known something was seriously wrong, but I didn't. I was so wrapped up in my own life and my own hurt feelings."

"It's not your fault. You didn't see her problems because she hid them from you. She shut you out of her life because she didn't want you to know about her troubles."

"I should have been there for her. Tried harder. I can't go back and fight for her. She's gone. But Hailey's here and I'm not going to give up on her. It's just the two of us. I can't lose her, too.

"I'm sorry for suggesting that you marry me. You're trying to do your job and I put you in an awkward position. It didn't help that in my frantic state I let you believe I was trying to force you."

"I understand. I know your heart was in the right place." The sorrow in Daniel's voice touched Brittany's heart. She came from a big family and couldn't imagine losing any of them, much less all but one of them. Holding on to that lone remaining family member might make her a little desperate, too. Who knew what crazy scheme she'd come up with if their positions were reversed? Maybe she would propose the same thing.

Brittany was no lawyer, so she didn't know the legal ins and outs of a custody case. Nor did she know what judges thought was important when making a decision. This judge might believe that a little girl needed a woman's influence. Right or wrong, wasn't that something most of society believed? Would a judge be any different? It hit her then. Though she didn't think he should lose the court case, there was a real chance that Daniel could lose the custody battle.

His voice broke into her thoughts. "Well, enough of my woes. I'll think of something. Let's look at what you have in mind for my dinner."

They tried to discuss Brittany's plans, but his heart didn't appear to be into it any more than hers was. Only Hailey, who was oblivious to the adult worries, was unbothered. She babbled happily to herself, setting the plastic rings on top of her head and then bending over and letting them slide off. When it became clear that they were each too distracted to focus, Brittany decided to leave the plans with him and suggested that they meet another day.

Daniel agreed and she gathered her belongings. Brittany went over to Hailey and scooped the little girl into her arms, giving her a long hug before handing her to Daniel. Since Brittany was leaving the material for Daniel to review, she wouldn't need to show up on his doorstep tomorrow morning. She might have only spent a little bit of time with Hailey, but the little girl had wiggled her way into Brittany's heart. She was going to miss her. And though she would definitely never say it out loud, Brittany was going to miss Daniel, too.

The rest of the day passed by in a blur and Brittany was glad to get home. She'd gotten a few questioning looks and more than one raised eyebrow when she'd told her coworkers she'd be skipping happy hour, but nobody pressed her for a reason. She was the furthest thing from happy and didn't think she could fake it. Daniel might believe she was a great actress, but she knew better. Her feelings always showed on her face.

She changed from her work clothes into a pair of shorts and a T-shirt before pouring a glass of wine and going outside to sit on her balcony. The weather was just perfect. Although her view was nowhere near as beautiful as Daniel's, it was still pleasant. Normally sitting out here and letting the cool evening breeze wash over her soothed her. Today the magic was lacking. After twenty minutes, she was still troubled. Still confused.

If she didn't know better, she'd think Daniel was trying to trick her into agreeing to marry him by appearing to back off. But she did know better. He took the direct approach. Besides, no one could fake that kind of agony. His heart was aching at the possibility of losing his little girl. Brittany had seen the way he was with Hailey. He adored her. And Hailey adored him right back. They belonged together.

So what was she going to do about it? Could she really live with herself if Hailey and Daniel were torn apart when she'd had the ability to prevent it? Hailey had already lost her parents before she was old enough to know them. She didn't deserve to lose Daniel, too.

And Daniel didn't deserve to lose his only remaining family member.

Muttering to herself that she was out of her mind, Brittany picked up her phone and dialed Daniel's number. When he answered, she didn't waste time with a greeting.

"I'll do it. I'll marry you."

Chapter Six

"Would you say that again?" Daniel asked. He needed confirmation that he hadn't imagined Brittany's words.

Her voice came over the phone loud and clear. "I said I'll marry you."

Relief surged through him, momentarily making him weak, and he sagged against his desk. "What changed your mind?"

"You and Hailey belong together. Anyone can see that. I want to do my part to even the odds. I would never forgive myself if you lost Hailey and I hadn't tried to help you."

His chest tightened and, for a minute, he

couldn't speak. He knew Brittany was a kind woman, but he'd begun to believe that marrying him so he could keep custody of Hailey had been too much of a sacrifice even for her. A part of him knew that his request was out of bounds. He wasn't going to retract it, though. Not if it meant losing Hailey.

"But I do have a condition."

"Name it. Anything you want is yours." He'd sign over his fortune if that's what she wanted.

"I'm renting a condo with a good friend. When I move, I want you to cover my share of the rent until our lease expires. I don't want to leave Amanda in the lurch."

"No problem. I'll give you a check for the balance of the rent immediately."

"What exactly are we going to tell people?" she asked.

"It's nobody's business."

"That may be true, but we have to tell them something. Otherwise they'll make up a story we might not want getting around."

"We'll tell people whatever you want."

She sighed. "Fine. We'll say it was a whirlwind courtship."

"Sounds good. How long will it take you to plan the wedding?"

"That depends on what you're looking for."

"You're the event planner, not me. Money is no object. I just want to get it over and done with."

Silence was her only reply and Daniel knew he'd made a mistake. Brittany understood that time was of the essence, but still, he could have been more tactful. "I didn't mean that the way it sounded."

She laughed, but it wasn't the joyous sound he'd heard on other occasions. "Of course you did. But it's fine. You're right. We do need to do this quickly. But since it's not going to be a real marriage, there's no need for an elaborate wedding. We can just get a license and get married at city hall."

She'd said all the right words, but he didn't get the sense that they'd come from her heart. Even though this was going to be a fake marriage, she was going to be a real bride. In the eyes of the law and everyone she knew, she was going to be his wife. As such, she deserved more than saying a few bland words in front of an indifferent judge.

"I think we can do better than that. What about a small party at DJ's Deluxe? We'll invite your family and our closest friends. How does that sound?"

"It sounds good. And speaking of family, you're going to have to meet mine. There's no way I can simply tell my parents I'm getting married to someone they've never met, no matter what kind of wedding we have. But if we have a ceremony, they have to be there. I can't get married without them."

"Of course not. Just name the time and the place."

"How about my parents' home on Sunday? The entire family gathers for dinner after church."

"The whole family? Just how many are we talking about?"

"My parents and my two brothers and two sisters. Sometimes a few aunts, uncles and cousins come by. But I'll ask my parents to limit it to just immediate family."

"I'd appreciate that." Brittany's family was a complication he hadn't considered. But if they were going to be convincing as a couple, he'd have to meet the in-laws.

"You can move in here after the ceremony. And although I've said it before, I'll say it anyway. There won't be a honeymoon or romantic wedding night. I hope that puts your mind at ease." Though he knew the marriage wouldn't be real, part of him regretted the fact that he wouldn't be sharing a bed with Brittany. She was a beautiful, sexy woman with a loving heart; the type of woman he'd want to marry if he ever chose to get married.

"It does."

The relief in her voice was proof her thoughts were miles away from his. He might find her desirable, but she was only marrying him to help him win the custody suit and to get seed money and recommendations for her business venture. This was a business arrangement. Sleeping together was the last thing on her mind. That was good. They didn't need the complications a sexual relationship would bring. Once he won the custody battle, they'd get an annulment and put the marriage behind them.

"Have you contacted a lawyer yet?" Daniel asked her. "We need to iron out the prenup. In my experience, having everything spelled out and in writing saves trouble down the line."

"I'm not after your money."

"I know that. But I still intend to uphold my end of the bargain. I offered you money to start your business and I intend to provide it. That's not negotiable. We both need to benefit from this deal."

"Okay. I'll hire someone to represent me."

"Thank you. What are you doing tomorrow?"

"Wednesday is my day off." She paused. "I have some errands to run, but nothing pressing. Why?"

"Can you meet me in town for lunch? We need to iron out the details."

"Isn't that what we're doing now?"

"Humor me," he quipped.

"Okay. I can always come by your ranch, if it's easier."

"No. We need to meet in Bronco."

"What about Hailey?" she asked. "You don't want people finding out about her."

"That can't be helped now. She's obviously going to be at the wedding. Besides, if we want to convince people our relationship is real, we need to be seen around town together. We might as well start now."

The doorbell pealed and Brittany jumped, which was a ridiculous reaction. Daniel had told her he'd be here at eleven thirty and it was eleven thirty on the nose. Telling herself to stop being foolish, she crossed the room and opened the door so Daniel, Hailey in his arms, could enter.

Despite telling herself that she wasn't interested in him romantically, her heart jumped at the sight of him. Dressed in a heather-gray shirt and black jeans, he looked ready to star in a romantic movie. His eyes lit up when he saw her and warmth flowed through her body in return.

Reminding herself that this was only make-believe, she stepped aside. "Come on in. I just need to grab my purse."

"Sure."

Daniel stepped inside and looked around. "Nice place."

"Thanks. I've been happy living here. Of course, the views from my balcony can't compete with those on your ranch."

"That's good to hear. Otherwise I would feel bad for pulling you away from your home and moving you to a ranch in the middle of nowhere."

Her home. Only now did she realize that she might not return to this condo after their marriage was annulled. Amanda could be married by then and living with Holt. Unless Brittany found a new roommate, she'd need to find a new place to live. But she'd made her decision and wasn't going to back out now. She'd worry about tomorrow's problems tomorrow.

She draped her purse strap over her shoulder then led them out the door.

When they were in his car, she turned to him. "So you said we had a stop to make before lunch. Where are we going?"

"The jewelry store."

"What? Why?"

"To get your engagement ring, of course."

"I don't need an engagement ring. A simple wedding band is more than enough."

"No way. There is absolutely no way we can convince anyone that our engagement is real if you aren't wearing a diamond. Anyone who knows me knows that I would give my fiancée an engagement ring."

"Maybe. But anyone who knows me knows I'm not a gold-digger."

"It's simply a ring. A tradition. No one will think anything bad about you for wearing it."

"Okay. But I don't want you to think that, either."

Daniel laughed. "Trust me, Brittany. As hard as I had to work to convince you to marry me, the thought never crossed my mind."

"Just so you know."

"I do. Consider the point made. Now let's get this show on the road."

Although Bronco wasn't the biggest town in Montana, it was quite wealthy. With affluent ranchers living nearby, and tourism that catered to the rich and famous, the town had several businesses that served those for whom money was no object. One such store was Beaumont and Rossi's Fine Jewels. The items sold there were exquisite and one of a kind, often personally designed. Brittany had saved up for months to purchase a pair of teardrop diamond earrings. Other than that one visit, she hadn't stepped foot inside the store.

When Daniel parked, she put a hand on his wrist, stopping him. "Are we really going to buy a ring here?"

"Of course."

"Do you know how much they cost?"

"I have an idea, yes."

Before she could protest, he was out of the

car and unstrapping Hailey from her car seat. With no choice but to follow, Brittany got out of the car then walked beside him. Acutely aware of the attention they were drawing, she pasted on a smile and tried not to think about the conversations that would be burning up the phone lines over the next hours. Though she would figure in them prominently, she knew most of the attention would be devoted to Daniel and the sweet baby in his arms.

The good citizens of Bronco had done their best to find out about Daniel, but the only knowledge anyone had gleaned had come from old media accounts. He'd done a spectacular job of keeping his personal life private. Now he was strolling down Bronco's Main Street with a baby in one arm and Brittany on the other. From the carefree way he smiled as they entered the jewelry store, he wasn't bothered by the scrutiny. Or perhaps that was part of his plan. The more people who saw the three of them together, the more believable their story would be. This was one scene in the play he was writing and Brittany was simply a bit actor.

A well-dressed gentleman approached them. "How may I help you?"

There were several other patrons admiring the jeweled creations, but other than glancing up to see who'd entered, they paid little attention to the newcomers.

"I have an appointment with Angelique. The name is Daniel Dubois."

"Of course. Follow me."

"An appointment?" Brittany whispered as they were whisked behind a curtain and into a private room.

"Yes. I've hired Angelique to design your ring. From what I've been told, she's one of the most talented designers in the country."

"Would you like a beverage?" the gentleman said in a cultured voice. "Juice for the baby?"

"No, thank you," Brittany said, replying for all of them. She took a seat on the plush sofa.

"Very good. Angelique will be right in." The man exited quietly.

Brittany looked around the elegant room. Gray silk curtains flanked the floor-to-ceiling windows and a gray-and-blue-patterned tapestry hung from the ceiling behind the enormous desk at the far end of the room. Vases of fresh flowers subtly perfumed the air.

A door opened and a willowy woman dressed in a black silk blouse and a black pencil skirt crossed the thick carpet until she stood in front of them. Her natural hair was styled in a massive curly afro. Silver earrings dangled from her ears. "How do you do? I'm Angelique. I'm pleased to be designing your wedding rings."

Brittany and Daniel introduced themselves. Daniel had brought a play mat for Hailey and he spread it on the floor while Brittany pulled several toys from the diaper bag. Hailey was content to play while the adults chatted.

"What kind of ring do you have in mind?"

Brittany glanced at Daniel. This was his show. He'd nixed her idea of a plain gold band, so she was going to let him take charge.

"Something original without being too

showy. Something beautiful and classy that demands attention without being ostentatious. Like my fiancée."

Daniel sounded so smitten that Brittany herself could almost believe he loved her.

"Are you looking for a diamond or another jewel?" Angelique asked. "Or a combination?"

Brittany shrugged. "I've never given thought to anything other than the traditional solitaire."

"Are we going with platinum?"

"Yes," Daniel replied before Brittany could say that gold would do.

"I'd like to ask a couple of questions about your relationship to get a sense of you as a couple. I'll design while we talk."

"You're going to come up with a ring just by listening to me?" Brittany was skeptical for a minute but then decided to give it a try. It wasn't too different from what she did as an event planner. From mere conversations with her client, she'd designed the most perfect parties. And if Angelique created something

Brittany didn't like, would it really matter? It wasn't as if Brittany planned to keep the ring. It was a prop in the play she and Daniel were producing and she planned to return it when their marriage was annulled.

"Yes." Angelique grabbed a sketchpad and pencils then smiled. "I'm ready when you are."

Brittany inhaled, then looked at Daniel. Suddenly she felt vulnerable, knowing she was about to reveal herself in front of him. She could lie, but why bother? It wasn't as if Daniel actually cared about the real her. She just fit the role of wife and mother he needed filled.

"Ask away," Brittany said.

"I'll start with something easy. What first attracted you to Daniel?"

"His body," Brittany replied without thinking. When she realized what she'd just said, her face heated and she made sure not to look in his direction.

"I see," Angelique said as she drew on the paper.

"But it was more than the way he looked. It was his presence. His confidence. His essence. He has a way of taking over a room, commanding attention without even trying."

"So does that makes you the power behind the throne?" Angelique asked, looking up.

"No."

"Yes," Daniel said instantly.

"Interesting," Angelique said with a knowing smile.

Just what was that supposed to mean?

"What is your relationship like?"

Whew. Brittany had no idea the questions were going to be like *this*. What ever happened to asking about her favorite color?

"It's fine," Brittany said and then winced. A generic store brand fake fiancée could do better than that. She took a breath and tried again. What would her perfect relationship with her imaginary fiancé be like? "It's good because we respect each other. We each have a strong personality, so that makes discussions interesting. But we respect each other, so our conversations are always fair."

"What is your dream for your life together?"

"To always be in love. To spend each day doing something to make the other happy and fulfilled. To work to make each other's dream a reality."

Brittany glanced over at Daniel. He was staring at her as if he'd never seen her before. Had she revealed too much? She certainly hoped not. This marriage was going to be in name only and she intended to keep each of her emotions to herself.

Angelique made a couple of marks on the pad and, with a flourish, turned it around to reveal the sketch.

Brittany took one look at the drawing and gasped in amazement. The ring was nothing short of spectacular. It was a beautiful sapphire surrounded by numerous diamonds. "It's perfect. Exactly what I would have pictured if I could have imagined it. Can you really make that?"

Angelique clapped her hands in obvious

glee. "I don't make the rings, but yes, the jeweler can make this for you."

"It is perfect," Daniel chimed in.

Angelique explained her design. "Listening to you talk, I knew that a simple elegant diamond, while beautiful, wouldn't capture your essence or that of your relationship with your fiancé. For you, I chose an oval-cut blue sapphire surrounded by round and marquis-cut diamonds. The design is inspired by the blue jasmine flower, which is a symbol of honesty and trust. The same qualities that are evident between the two of you. The blue jasmine also symbolizes that a woman is ready to give her heart to that special someone, as you clearly are."

Brittany suddenly felt uneasy. Apparently, she'd played the role of devoted fiancée a little too well. And now she was going to be stuck wearing a ring that symbolized a lie.

She knew she should have gotten a basic diamond that didn't stand for anything. Or better yet, she should have stuck to her guns and insisted on a plain gold band. It was too late now. There was no turning back.

"When can the ring be ready?" Daniel asked.

"It can take between two and four weeks."

"No. That's too long. We'd like to be married before then, so we need to expedite the process. Money is no object, so your store will be generously compensated."

Angelique's eyes darted to Brittany's flat stomach before returning to Daniel's eyes. "Of course. I'll speak with the jeweler right away. I shouldn't be more than a moment."

"She thinks I'm pregnant," Brittany said when the woman left.

"Does it matter?"

"It will when word reaches my parents."

"We're having dinner with them this Sunday. Surely the gossips won't beat us there. Besides, I can't imagine she'd risk losing our business by spreading baseless gossip."

"You could be right."

"I am."

The conversation ended with the arrival of

the jeweler. He introduced himself as Amos Rossi and he immediately assured Daniel that the ring would be made in record time without sacrificing quality.

"If you want to sign off on the design now, I can put together a selection of sapphires and diamonds for you to choose from. They'll be ready for your review in two hours, if that suits you. You can choose the ones you like and I can begin work on your ring immediately."

"That works for us," Daniel said.

Apparently, they were doing this.

Brittany put Hailey's toys into the diaper bag as the baby began to fuss.

"Hailey and I will go for a little walk outside while you wrap up the details," Brittany told Daniel then looked at Angelique and Mr. Rossi. "It was very nice meeting both of you."

She hurried through the store, hoping to make it outside without attracting too much attention. Hailey liked the faster pace and her fussing turned into giggles.

There was a wrought-iron bench a short

distance from the jewelry store, so Brittany headed there. She sat then stood Hailey on her lap. Gurgling happily, the baby bounced up and down.

Ten minutes later, Daniel joined them, sitting beside Brittany. "Would you like to get something to eat or would you rather do more shopping?"

"Shopping for what?" What else did he think she needed?

"Your wedding dress, of course."

"I'm not the superstitious type, but I believe it's bad luck for the groom to see the bride in the wedding dress ahead of time. Besides, I'm perfectly capable of picking out my own dress."

"I'll pay for it."

"No, you won't. I have money of my own."

"I'm sure you do. But I don't see why you should bear that burden when you're doing me the favor."

"It's not a favor." Calling it a favor gave the appearance that they were friends instead of business associates. There was nothing personal between them and she'd better not forget it. "We have a deal, remember? I get my business out of this. I consider the dress as one of my expenses." Her voice came out sharper than she'd intended, and Daniel winced.

"What's wrong?"

"Nothing." Nothing other than the fact that for a brief moment she'd lost control of her feelings and revealed more than she'd wanted. To him and to herself.

"You seem upset."

"I'm not." How could she explain that designing the wedding ring had been something she could only fantasize about? This whole fake marriage was becoming more confusing by the minute. And they hadn't even spoken their vows yet.

She'd gotten swept up in the emotional moment, forgetting that the ring didn't symbolize their promise of love. It had been all too easy to pretend that the romance they were perpetrating was real. But it wasn't. If

Brittany wasn't careful, she would end up with hurt feelings at best and a broken heart at worst.

Chapter Seven

Brittany paced her apartment all the while telling herself to relax. Taking a deep breath, she counted to three and then slowly blew it out, then checked her appearance in the mirror. It wouldn't do to look stressed today of all days. She was taking Daniel to meet her family in a few minutes. Not only were her parents living lie detectors, but her siblings would also be able to pick up on her stress. The last thing she needed was to make any of them suspicious.

She'd chosen to wear a simple pink-and-orange sleeveless cotton floral dress with an orange short-sleeved cropped sweater. Although dinners at her parents' house was always casual, she'd felt the need to be a little dressier today. After all, she was arriving with her fiancé.

Her doorbell rang and she squared her shoulders. She could do this.

She opened the door and Daniel stood there, holding Hailey in his arms. When the baby saw Brittany, she babbled a few syllables and reached out to her. Though Brittany had no intention of having children of her own, there was something about Hailey's joy at seeing her that warmed Brittany's heart and made her smile. Taking the tyke from Daniel, she led them into her living room. Hailey strained to get down, so Brittany set her on the floor.

"I'm ready to go. I just need to get my purse," Brittany said.

"Actually, let's sit down a minute." His voice didn't sound as confident as it usually did, and a sliver of worry crawled down her spine.

"Okay." She sat on the sofa and Daniel sat

beside her. Unbothered, Hailey sat at their feet and pushed buttons on her musical toy turtle. "What's up?"

Daniel tapped his foot three times. He sucked in a breath and patted his knee. She didn't know why he was suddenly nervous, but he was stressing her out.

"Okay," he said softly, and she wondered whether he was talking to her or his invisible friend. He cleared his throat, then stood. A heartbeat later he knelt in front of her and took her hand in his.

Wait. Was he? *Oh my goodness.* He was. Her heart skipped a beat, then began to race.

"Brittany, I know that we have not known each other long and that this isn't going to be a traditional marriage, but I promise to be the best husband that I know how. I'll always respect you and support your dreams. I'll help you to become your best self." He inhaled and his shirt tightened over his muscular chest. "Will you do me the honor of becoming my wife?"

Her heart stuttered and suddenly she was

just as tongue-tied as he'd been only moments ago. Sure, he was really proposing, but it was for a fake marriage. One with an expiration date. But when he looked into her eyes, the sincerity there touched her heart. This wasn't real, so why was her vision suddenly blurry?

She realized he was waiting for an answer. "Yes." Her voice was barely audible, so she cleared her throat and tried again. "Yes. Yes, I'll marry you."

Daniel pulled the ring from his pocket and slid it onto her ring finger. It fit perfectly. Although it didn't weigh much, wearing it she suddenly felt the gravity of the situation.

She and Daniel were engaged.

Daniel stood and scooped Hailey into his arms. "Ready to go?"

Brittany blinked at the quick change in his attitude. It was as if they'd been filming a movie and someone had yelled "cut." The emotional atmosphere had dissipated, and he was on to the next thing, leaving her off balance.

But why was she suddenly so disconcerted?

She'd known all along this was a business-arrangement marriage. She shouldn't expect love or romance, even with the marriage proposal. Besides, she hadn't been expecting one until he'd gotten down on his knee.

Telling herself to snap out of it, she rose, grabbed her purse and then pasted on a smile. "I'm ready. Let's go."

Brittany twisted the engagement ring on her finger, turning the stone to the inside against her palm before turning it back the right way with the sapphire back on top. She'd been fiddling with her ring the entire ride to her parents' home. From the way she was behaving, you would think she was the one about to try to convince her soon-to-be in-laws that she was good enough to marry their child and not the other way around.

"You want to stop that? You're making me nervous." Daniel had been doing his best to maintain a calm facade, but his stomach, which had been bubbling since this morning, had started churning wildly as the day passed. Now it felt as if he had a volcano inside him. But since Brittany was clearly stressed about the meeting, he'd done his best to appear confident.

When she looked at him, a question on her face, he was struck once again by her beauty. With clear, light brown skin and large brown eyes and kissable lips, she could easily be on the cover of a fashion magazine. When they'd initially met, he'd tried to ignore her sexy, willowy body and her stunning good looks, but hadn't been successful. He had even less chance of ignoring her beauty now that he'd trashed his policy of not becoming personally involved with women he did business with. They were going to be married even if in name only.

"What am I doing?"

"You're playing with your ring."

"Sorry." She placed her hands in her lap and spread her fingers. "This entire situation feels a little bit surreal. I can't believe that we're actually pretending to be engaged."

"Stop right there. We aren't *pretending*

to be engaged. We *are* engaged. And we're going to be getting married in two weeks."

They'd managed to snag DJ's Deluxe's private party room for that date. Ordinarily, getting reservations on such short notice was nearly impossible, but Daniel had money and money opened otherwise closed doors. The wedding would be lavish yet intimate. Daniel had wanted to leave the details to Brittany, but she'd insisted on his involvement, pointing out that he was the one who wanted to get married.

"You know what I mean," she said.

"I do. But you can't slip up like that. If anyone ever suspects that we aren't really in love, it could be detrimental to my case."

"I know. You're right."

"Do you like the ring?" he asked.

She sighed and held her left hand in front of her. "Too much. It is so beautiful."

Knowing she was pleased made it worth every penny. Not that he cared about the money. "They did a good job."

Even Hailey's happy chatter in the car hadn't been enough to calm his nerves. When the door had swung open and Hailey had seen Brittany, she'd squealed with delight and lunged for her. Brittany had scooped the baby into her arms and kissed her chubby cheeks then smiled at him. His heart had leaped with joy at the sight of the two of them together. After he'd stepped inside, Brittany had settled Hailey on the floor with her toys.

He'd taken Brittany gently by the arm and led her to the couch. Then he'd taken her hand into his. Her fingers had trembled and, admitting to feeling a bit more emotional that he'd expected as he'd proposed, told himself, *This isn't real.*

The ring had fit perfectly. She'd gasped audibly before pulling her hand away from his. He hadn't wanted to release her and had struggled not to reach out and take hold of her hand again. The longing he'd felt to renew the contact had surprised him and was enough to have him jumping to his feet.

They'd left her condo shortly thereafter to go to her parents' house.

Now he couldn't stop thinking about the Brandt relatives he was about to meet. "Tell me about your family."

"What do you want to know?"

"Anything. Pretend like we were dating and you're sharing stories about how you grew up. Tell me things you would tell your fiancé. The last thing I want is for your family to have doubts about our relationship. I want them to believe we're in love. Or have you changed your mind about letting them in on our secret?"

"No. My parents are traditional. They believe in the sanctity of marriage. They were high school sweethearts and got married when they were twenty-one. If I tell them this marriage is only pretend, they wouldn't approve."

She clasped her hands and shifted toward him in her seat. "My father is the superintendent of the Sunday school and my mother sings in the choir. They're very close."

"Yeah, I'm picking up on that."

"They work together, so they spend just about every minute of every day with each other. They own a dry-cleaning business. They started out with one and now own fifteen locations throughout Montana."

"That had to take a lot of work."

"Yes. And while they were building the business, I was tasked with caring for my four younger brothers and sisters."

Her voice was dry and he might have heard a hint of bitterness. Did she resent her siblings? He'd give anything to have Jane back in his life. Taking care of her daughter was a joy and privilege. Clearly, Brittany didn't look at family the same way he did. Maybe he didn't know her as well as he'd thought. For that reason alone, he needed to remember that this was a fake relationship and that he had to take control of his physical attraction to her.

Brittany directed him to turn at the next corner and then into the third driveway on the left. The house was well kept and the lawn immaculate. Once they were out of the car, Brittany turned to him. "Thanks for doing this. I know meeting my family isn't part of our deal, but it's important to me."

"If it's important to you, then it's important to me." She smiled at him and the pleasure in her expression made his blood race. Hadn't he just told himself to keep a tight rein on his desire? "Besides, whirlwind romance or not, it would look really strange if I didn't meet your family before the wedding."

Her smile vanished. "You're right. We don't want to do anything that would make the judge suspicious."

He replayed his words in his mind and couldn't think of anything he'd said that would account for the change in her attitude. Perhaps she was just nervous. He was.

They climbed the stairs together and then Brittany rang the doorbell. She didn't wait for anyone to answer the bell, but opened the door and stepped inside. Deciding that it would be odd not to follow suit, he stepped inside, too.

The delicious aroma of greens and candied yams filled the air and his mouth began to water. He couldn't remember the last time he'd had authentic soul food. Definitely not since he'd moved to Montana. His cook had received training at the best school in the country and had studied in France, but the man couldn't make spaghetti casserole to save his life. As much as Daniel enjoyed fancy food, there was nothing like fried turkey and baked macaroni and cheese to make a man feel good.

"We're here," Brittany called.

"Hi. Did Amanda come with you?" a woman asked, stepping into the room. It only took one look for Daniel to identify her as Brittany's mother.

"No. I brought someone else. Two 'some-ones' actually." Brittany sounded a bit nervous and he reached out and grabbed her hand, giving it a gentle squeeze. She smiled at him and his heart squeezed in response.

"I see." Brittany's mother looked at Daniel,

who was holding Hailey in his arms, and then back to Brittany. "And who have we here?"

"Mom, this is Daniel Dubois and this little sweetheart is Hailey."

"It's a pleasure to meet you, Mrs. Brandt."

"Call me Mallory."

Before Daniel could respond, two black Labs bounded into the room and Brittany bent to greet each of them.

"Baba," Hailey exclaimed, kicking her legs in an attempt to get down.

"Are they friendly?" Daniel asked Mallory.

"Yes."

Daniel was considering the best way to deal with the Labs when an enormous dog thundered into the room, knocking into a floor lamp, which teetered momentarily.

"Do not tell me Lucas brought that gigantic mutt of his," Brittany said.

"Hey, don't insult my baby," a man said, coming into the room. "You'll hurt his feelings."

"I'll hurt more than that if he drools on me. I still can't believe Daphne let you rescue a mastiff, of all things. She should have given you a cat." Brittany made a mental note to speak to her friend, who ran the Happy Hearts Animal Rescue shelter, the next time she saw her.

"I'm a dog man. Besides, Flash is my baby, aren't you, girl?"

"You're a mess," Brittany said, but with great affection.

"Hi. I'm Lucas, Brittany's brother," he said, offering his hand to Daniel.

"Daniel."

They shook and Lucas turned around and yelled over his shoulder, "Brittany brought a man with her. And a baby."

"What are you, the town crier?" Brittany grumbled, and her brother only laughed.

In the blink of an eye, the rest of Brittany's family filled the room. An older gentleman elbowed his way to the front. "Give the man some space. You'll likely scare him off crowding around him like that." When he reached Daniel, he smiled and held out his hand. "I'm Phillip Brandt, Brittany's father. And father to the rest of this unruly bunch."

Daniel introduced himself and Hailey, who was clinging to him, her interest in the dogs a thing of the past. Apparently, six additional people was more than she wanted to deal with.

"These are my sisters, Stephanie and Tiffany, and my other brother, Ethan," Brittany said. As she introduced her siblings, they smiled or nodded at him. Brittany's sisters shared her slender build, hair and eye color as well as her skin tone. They were quite pretty, but in his estimation, Brittany was by far the most beautiful of the three.

"You're right on time. We were about to put dinner on the table," her mother said. "And, Lucas, put the dogs outside. Can't you see that horse of yours is scaring the baby?"

Hailey looked around at the word "horse." She might not know how to talk, but she was beginning to understand the meaning of words. *Horse* was one she was clued up on.

Brittany led him into the dining room where

Phillip was setting up a high chair. Brittany must have sensed Daniel's confusion because she replied to his unasked question. "A couple of my cousins have kids. Since they come over for dinner quite often, my mother has a high chair."

Once the chair was set up, Brittany took Hailey from his arms and placed her in the chair. When she was securely strapped in, Brittany dropped a kiss onto her forehead.

There were two minutes of absolute chaos as food was carried into the room and set on the table. Brittany's family bumped into each other, and there was some good-natured grumbling and fussing until the table was so full he doubted another serving bowl would fit. When everyone was seated, they joined hands for a quick grace. Once finished, they began to pass platters of food. He scooped macaroni and cheese onto his plate then turned to pass the dish to Brittany's brother, who was seated beside him. A shriek had him pausing in the action, holding the casserole in the air.

"What is that on your finger?" Stephanie asked, grabbing Brittany's hand and holding it out so everyone could see. He felt Brittany stiffen beside him.

The moment of truth had arrived.

Chapter Eight

Brittany gave him a rueful look, then turned to face her sister. "It's a ring. Why, what does it look like?"

"It's on your *left* hand."

"Your powers of observation are nothing short of astounding."

"Brittany." Stephanie's voice was part whine and part excitement.

"Okay. Daniel and I are engaged."

There was a moment of silence before the women all screamed. Then everyone began to talk at once. Her mother jumped up and ran around the table, giving Brittany a big hug. She then did the same to Daniel. After the commotion died down, people once more began to fill their plates.

"That wasn't too bad," Daniel whispered. "I thought there would be a lot more questions than that."

Brittany smiled internally. He was so wrong. He really had no idea what was about to hit them. Still, Brittany hoped the questions wouldn't come until after dessert.

"So how did the two of you meet and when did all of this happen?" her mother asked.

Brittany sighed as that hope went sailing out the window. She glanced at Daniel, who shrugged. She hated lying to her family, but it was the better of two bad options. She didn't want to make them accomplices to her deception. Especially when she knew how much they disliked lies.

Her parents had drilled the importance of honesty into her at a young age. Her father had emphasized that you only got one name. One reputation. If you ruined it by lies or other bad behavior, you had to live with the consequences. He'd given each of his kids a good name and would appreciate if they kept it that way.

She couldn't count the number of times her mother had reminded her that if you told the truth, you didn't have to worry about keeping your story straight. Those words had never rung truer. The plan she and Daniel had agreed upon was to stick to the truth when possible, limiting the risk of being tripped up.

"We met when Daniel hired me to plan an event for him. I took one look at him and wham. The feelings knocked me right between the eyes. It was kismet."

"I'm not surprised," her mother said. "I knew it would be that way for you. You were always so certain that you didn't want to get married and have kids. So focused on your career. And look at you now." She glanced at Hailey, who was feeding herself smashed macaroni and cheese and mixed greens. Just as much was ending up on her face and in her hair as in her mouth, but Brittany was still proud of the little girl.

"So when is the date?" Stephanie asked.

Brittany blew out a breath. "Actually, we're planning to get married soon."

"Vague much?" Tiffany said.

Brittany nudged Daniel with her shoulder. A little help would be nice. He must have gotten the message, because he chimed in. "I convinced Brittany to set the date for the Saturday after next."

"What? That soon?" Her mom's shriek was nearly drowned out by the rest of the family. Used to the commotion, Brittany kept eating as they talked over each other. She looked at Daniel, concerned that he was rattled by the racket, but he appeared unfazed as he took a second helping of macaroni and cheese. Pleased by his reaction, Brittany smiled.

When the conversation ended, Daniel looked at Brittany's family. "I guess I'm a little bit impatient. But when you meet the right one, you don't want to wait."

"What about Hailey's mother?" Mallory asked.

"She died." Daniel's voice was ragged, and

Brittany heard the pain there. She placed her hand on his and gave it a gentle squeeze.

"I'm so sorry to hear that." Her mother's voice was filled with genuine sorrow, as was everyone else's who echoed her comments. "Were you married long?"

"We weren't married at all."

"Oh." Brittany's parents exchanged a look.

This was just as hard as Brittany had expected.

"Jane, Hailey's mother, was my younger sister," Daniel said quietly. "She died in a car accident recently. She asked that I raise Hailey as my daughter and that's what I intend to do."

"I see," Mallory said quietly. Brittany could only wonder what it was her mother saw. Did she suspect that Brittany and Daniel weren't being entirely truthful? Was she now having doubts about whether the upcoming marriage was a good idea?

"It takes a good man to take on the responsibility of a baby." Phillip's voice was filled with approval.

"I love Hailey. It might not be legal yet, but she's my daughter now, in my heart."

"Of course she is," Mallory said before turning to Brittany. "So what kind of dress are you going to wear?"

That was it? No talk about Brittany's new role as stepmother?

"Can we not talk about the wedding until after we eat?" Lucas pleaded.

"I second that motion," Ethan said. "Just hearing the word is making my stomach turn and I won't be able to do justice to this great food. Everything tastes delicious, Mom, by the way."

Mallory blew her youngest child a kiss.

"We'll stop talking about the wedding if you guys agree to clean up the kitchen," Tiffany said.

"Fine," Lucas said as Ethan nodded. "Anything not to have to talk about lace and beads."

After that, conversation switched to other topics. Brittany was pleased by the way her siblings included Daniel and even ribbed him good-naturedly. He seemed to enjoy the banter and gave as good as he got. If ever she found Mr. Right, she'd want him to fit in with her family just as well as Daniel did.

When dinner was done, Lucas and Ethan kept their word and cleared the dishes. The women teased them before they went into the living room to continue discussing the wedding.

"Let's talk in my office," Phillip said, clapping a hand on Daniel's shoulder.

"Sure." Daniel looked at Hailey, who was now lying across Mallory's lap. As the dinner had progressed, Hailey had grown tired of sitting in her high chair and had started to fuss. Daniel had taken her out of the chair, ready to hold her, but Mallory had taken her, saying that Hailey needed to become familiar with the rest of her family. Throughout the meal, Hailey had spent time on everyone's lap. Brittany had no doubt that the little girl was going to be spoiled in no time.

"Go. She'll be fine," Mallory said. "I've raised five of my own, so I know a thing or two about babies. Besides, Brittany is here if Hailey needs to see a familiar face."

Brittany watched as Daniel followed her father out of the room. Her mother patted her hand. "He'll be fine."

"I know," Brittany replied. Phillip was a gentle man who loved his family. As long as Brittany was happy, he would be happy.

"This is kind of sudden," her mother said softly so that her words reached Brittany's ears alone. She should have known her mother wouldn't let the timing issue drop easily.

"I know. But it feels right to me."

"I raised you to know your own mind and make your own decisions. You've done a good job to date. I'm not going to try to run your life now, so stop frowning at me before your face freezes that way. If you think getting married this soon is right for you, then it's fine by me. Now, let's talk about colors."

After that, Brittany was able to completely relax. Unlike most teenagers or women in their twenties, she'd never imagined her dream wedding. And, oddly enough for an event planner, she was stumped when it came to planning her own wedding. Perhaps it was because she didn't want to be surrounded by the symbols of love and devotion when she and Daniel weren't devoted to each other. And they certainly weren't in love. Heck, a week ago, she wasn't even sure she liked him. She'd grown to admire him, but admiration was a long way away from being in love.

Could she really go with pink hyacinths when they symbolized happiness and love? Or pink peonies, which meant romance and a happy marriage? Not a chance. And she certainly couldn't use dahlias knowing they symbolized commitment and honesty. Nothing about this wedding was honest.

"How about tulips?" Tiffany suggested.

"Yes, you love tulips," her mother added.

She did. But tulips were a symbol of perfect love. She wanted to say no as she had to magenta lilacs and their love and passion, but she didn't want to raise suspicions by being difficult. And, really, who else knew the symbolism behind the flowers? Definitely not her sisters.

"Okay. I like that idea."

"What about bridesmaids?" Stephanie asked.

"I want each of you to stand up with me, of course. And Amanda."

"Yes." Stephanie cheered, clapping her hands.

"I was hoping you were going to say that," Tiffany said. "What color dresses are we going to wear?"

"What color would you like?"

The sisters talked excitedly to each other, coming up with and then discarding several colors as too bold, too boring, too...something.

"Well?" Brittany asked when they'd finally stopped talking.

They grinned at each other before speaking in unison. "Pink."

Brittany laughed. Her sisters knew pink was her favorite color. Not because she was a froufrou girl. She'd just always liked it. And each of her sisters looked fantastic in pink. Of course, they looked good in everything.

All the laughter and chatting had Hailey stirring and she sat up and looked around. At that moment, Lucas and Ethan returned to the room. Hailey took one look at Lucas and began to bounce on Mallory's lap and clap her hands. Then she raised her arms and stretched her little body as she tried to reach him. With rich brown skin and pretty-boy good looks, Lucas appealed to females from eight to eighty-eight. Apparently, that number should be lowered to eight months since Hailey wasn't immune to his charm, either.

"Hey, sweetie. Want to hang out with Uncle Lucas?" He reached out and swept her into his arms then settled her on his shoulders. Hailey squealed in delight and grabbed his locs. Laughing, he went down on his hands and knees to give her a horsey ride. Hailey bellowed with laughter and kicked her legs as if urging him to go faster, so he did.

"You'd better slow down," Brittany warned.

"Why? She likes it." Lucas began bucking like bronco, which delighted Hailey even more and she laughed raucously. "See? I'm totally going to be her favorite uncle."

"When she spits up all over your head, don't say anything."

"What's a little spit between friends?" he asked. He did, however, get to his feet and lower Hailey from his shoulders. He held her against his chest and looked into her eyes. "You wouldn't spit up on Uncle Lucas now, would you?"

Hailey just laughed.

"Looks like she isn't making any promises. Smart girl," Stephanie said.

Lucas winked. "We have a bond that doesn't require words."

Brittany watched the interaction between her siblings then glanced at her watch. She nibbled on her bottom lip.

"Why do you look so worried all of a sudden?" Stephanie asked.

"I'm just wondering what Dad and Daniel have been talking about all this time."

"Dad is probably threatening him within

an inch of his life," Ethan said, cleaning his glasses on his pressed button-down shirt before returning them to his face. "You know, telling him how you're his precious daughter and that he'd better treat you like gold or else."

"No way. Dad is probably telling him to run while he can," Lucas joked. "Brittany has been known to be bossy."

"Good thing you're holding the baby, or you would be toast," Brittany said.

"Would you two stop?" her mother said, clearly exasperated. "Your father and Daniel are just getting to know each other."

"Get away while you still can," Lucas said, laughing.

"Brat." But Brittany laughed. Her mother was probably right. So why couldn't she shake the mental image of her father chasing her fake fiancé?

Daniel fought back the ridiculous nerves churning his stomach. He and Phillip were going to have a simple talk. Daniel talked to people all of the time. This shouldn't be any different. But it was. Because this wasn't a talk between friends or business associates. This was a man-to-man talk between a man and his future father-in-law. True, the marriage between Daniel and Brittany wasn't going to be a real one, and Daniel didn't expect it to last long. But Phillip didn't know that. He believed Daniel and Brittany were going to be together for the rest of their lives.

Now that he'd met the Brandts and he and Hailey had been enveloped into her family, Daniel understood why Brittany hadn't wanted to tell them the truth. They were honest and open people who wouldn't be comfortable with the deceit. Though she'd tried to hide it, Daniel could tell that Brittany wasn't at ease with the deception, either. But because she wanted to help him, she was willing to compromise her morals.

"Don't look so nervous," Phillip said with a grin. "This won't be painful. I just want to get to know you better. It's easier to talk privately. You and Brittany are going to be getting married in a couple of weeks, so that doesn't give us much time."

"True. What do you want to know about me?"

Phillip laughed. "This isn't a job interview. I don't have a list of questions to ask you. Truth be told, I wasn't expecting to meet you today. When Brittany said she was bringing a guest to dinner, I thought she meant Amanda. It turns out she meant her fiancé and her future daughter."

"You didn't refer to Hailey as Brittany's future stepdaughter."

Leaning back in his leather chair, Phillip crossed his arms over his stomach and raised an eyebrow. "You didn't refer to her as your niece, either."

"True. I don't think of her that way. I think of her as my daughter."

"There you have it." Phillip nodded his head, as if that explained everything. And in a way it did. To the Brandts, family was family. That was why they'd opened their arms and their hearts to him and Hailey.

A lump sprouted in Daniel's throat and he had to swallow before speaking. This was what he wanted for Hailey. He wanted to raise her as his daughter, like he'd sworn he would. But more than that, he wanted to give her a loving family. Of course, this family would disappear once he gained legal custody of Hailey and he and Brittany split, but in the meantime, she would be loved beyond his greatest imagining.

Phillip crossed his legs. He fired off a few questions to get the conversation rolling but, true to his word, the talk was genial, relaxed. "So you want to open a guest ranch?" he finally asked.

"Yes. That's actually how Brittany and I met. I hired her firm to plan a dinner for me. Needless to say, she made quite the impression on me."

"That's Brittany. I was beginning to think she was so focused on her career that she wouldn't ever consider getting married and having a family. It turns out she was waiting for the right man." After a moment, Phillip stood and extended a hand. "I'm glad to know you. Welcome to the family."

Inexplicably, the lump returned to Daniel's throat. He wasn't normally sentimental, but over the past few hours at the Brandts', he'd found himself growing emotional. The last few years had been rough on him. He'd lost his parents and sister, leaving him with only Hailey as his family. His family might not have been as big or affectionate as this one, but they'd loved each other in their own way. He hadn't realized just how alone he'd been before Hailey had come into his life. Now he had the Brandts, too. At least for the duration of his marriage to Brittany.

"Thank you. You have a great family."

"I think so, but then I'm biased. They'll be your family soon, too. Now, let's get out of here. I'd like to spend a little bit more time spoiling my new granddaughter. And another piece of German chocolate cake wouldn't hurt."

Daniel followed his future father-in-law into the living room. The sight that greeted him made him smile. Brittany and her sisters were sitting on the sofa, their heads together as they talked a mile a minute. Mallory was sitting in a chair beside them, nodding as she typed into her laptop. Wedding planning was apparently in full swing.

Brittany glanced up at him and smiled. He felt the strangest twinge in his chest as his breath caught. She was so beautiful; he could have looked at her all night. But her beauty wasn't limited to the physical. She had the most gorgeous heart of anyone he'd ever met.

Hailey was sitting on a blanket, banging on a metal bowl with a wooden spoon and "singing" along. He scooped her up and gave her a big kiss. "That's a bit noisy. How about we give it a rest?"

The women just laughed. Clearly, they hadn't been bothered by the noise.

"The guys are in the kitchen getting more dessert, if you want to join them," Brittany said. "Or you could help us with the planning. It's your wedding, too."

"Whatever you decide is fine with me."

"Besides, there's cake and coffee in the kitchen," Tiffany teased.

"Yep."

"We'll be done soon," Brittany promised.

"Take your time," Daniel said, stepping out and joining the male members of the Brandt family. The day was turning out better than he'd expected, and he was actually having fun. He didn't have a problem with enjoying himself a little while longer. After all, he knew it was going to end soon.

Perhaps too soon?

Chapter Nine

"I really enjoyed myself today," Daniel said. "I'm glad I got to meet your family."

"They loved you," Brittany said honestly. Though she'd been the one who'd wanted them to meet, she'd been worried about their reaction to him and news of her upcoming wedding. She should have known her family would welcome him and Hailey with open arms. He'd fit right in and had become fast friends with her brothers. When she and mother had hugged at the door before they'd left, Mallory had whispered in her ear, "Daniel's a good man. You've chosen well." Her mother's words had filled Brittany with unexpected pride and warmth. Her mother had always wanted Brittany to find the same joy in marriage that she herself had found. Brittany didn't want to think about how disappointed her mother would be when she found out the truth. But since Brittany had gone into this with her open eyes she would deal with her mother's reaction when the time came.

"I loved them, too."

They'd finally gotten Hailey down for the night. After her busy day, she'd splashed for a long time in her bath before calming down enough to let Brittany wash her, then dress her in footed pajamas and rock her to sleep. Brittany had been surprised by how natural it had felt to hold the little girl and sing her a lullaby. But considering that Hailey was about to become her temporary daughter, it was a good development.

Daniel and Brittany were sitting in his very masculine living room. The curtains were open and moonlight streamed through the windows, making the large room feel intimate.

She shifted, brushing against Daniel's shoulder. They both froze. Until this moment she hadn't realized how close they were sitting. Suddenly there was a shift in the atmosphere and Brittany felt a oneness with Daniel that she'd never felt with anyone else. She certainly hadn't expected to feel it with him. The bond that she'd been pretending to share with him was starting to feel real. That was a problem. She needed to draw a bright line between what was real and what was fake.

She took a reluctant breath. "I guess I should be getting home."

"So soon?" He sounded shocked and maybe a little bit disappointed. No, she had to be imagining that. Why would he be disappointed? "I was hoping you could stay awhile. I could make some coffee to go with the cake."

Brittany laughed. Mallory had sent home two large pieces of cake, along with a plate of leftovers. "I'll just take the coffee. You can keep my piece of cake."

"You sure?"

She nodded.

He placed a hand over his heart and stared into her eyes. "You're the best."

Brittany's heart did a silly little lurch and she cautioned herself to calm down. His words didn't mean anything. He was just glad to have an extra dessert. Still, it was foolish to deny the way she'd reacted. Not one for lying—present situation excepted—she forced herself to acknowledge her attraction to him while simultaneously making up her mind not to let it grow.

How pitiful would it be to allow herself to fall for someone she knew had no intention of returning the feeling? Daniel had made it clear that theirs was now and always would be a business relationship. And since she wasn't really the maternal type and wasn't looking to marry anytime in the near future, why was she so bothered?

Daniel was back in a minute, holding two mugs, one with a plate balanced on top. He offered her the solitary mug and then set the other on the table.

She took a sip of her coffee. "Delicious."

"Thanks." He settled back on the sofa beside her, grabbed the plate and fork, and then took a bite of cake. Leaning back, he closed his eyes, savoring the treat. She had never found the way a man chewed especially sexy, but she was slightly turned on by watching Daniel devour his cake. She licked her lips as she imagined his lips on hers and the pleasure they would both get from kissing.

"So, do you want to talk more about the wedding?" she said, suddenly warm. She needed to focus on something other than how sexy his lips were and how badly she wanted to feel them on hers.

"Sure. What did you guys come up with?"

"My sisters will be my bridesmaids. And I'm going to ask Amanda to be my maid of honor. Do you have three close friends who can stand up for you?"

"Yes. I'll ask my friends Sam and Dominick to be groomsmen and my best friend, Stephanos, to be my best man."

"Are you going to have a bachelor party? If so, I can keep Hailey for you."

"I don't think so. The four of us will probably just get together the night they arrive and go to dinner or something. Of course, I have to tell them I'm getting married first."

She grinned. "What are you waiting for? Scared of what they'll say? Or has reality hit you? Are you scared of turning in your bachelor card?"

"Not hardly."

"I did a little checking on you. Before you moved here, you were considered one of the Southwest's most eligible bachelors. There were dozens of pictures of you with beautiful women. Emphasis on the word *women*. You were frequently photographed with a beautiful woman on your arm, but rarely the same woman twice. Maybe your friends won't believe you're ready to settle down with one woman. Especially with someone like me."

He turned and she felt the full force of his gaze. "Someone like you? Just what does that mean?"

"I live in Bronco, Montana. That's hardly a bustling metropolis. I'm an event planner, not a fashion model or actress—the type of woman you normally date. I'm a regular person with a regular job."

"You could be a model if you wanted to. You're just as beautiful as any of them."

She smiled. He thought she was beautiful? She'd never given much thought to her looks. Genes were inherited and thus not something that one could claim as an accomplishment. From a young age, she had been taught a person wasn't beautiful because of how they looked, but rather because of how he or she behaved. Brittany believed that and always tried to be kind. Still... *Daniel thought she was beautiful.*

"Thank you," she managed to say. "But that's not my point. I don't live a jet-set life. I don't mingle with celebrities and millionaires. My nights out are spent with friends at a local restaurant. And I'm all right with that."

"So am I." He leaned forward. "If I wanted

to live life in the fast lane, I wouldn't have moved to Bronco. Although I enjoyed the life I had, I want to live a slower life now. I want to have a horse ranch and resort. That's why I moved here."

She nodded. It sounded believable when he said it.

"And if I wanted to, I could have married one of those women. But I don't want them. I want you."

A tingle raced down her spine and once more she was in danger of being swept away by his words. Her heart sped up as she thought of how great it would be if he'd really meant them. How fabulous it would be for him to want *her*, not just a woman who would fool a judge. What would it be like to be the woman Daniel actually chose to marry because he loved her? She cleared her throat and focused. Daydreaming was dangerous to her heart. And her goals. "Speaking of the wedding…"

"I told you. I'm happy with whatever you come up with."

"I know. But we haven't talked specifically about the marriage."

"Okay." He looked at her expectantly, waiting for her to continue.

"I want to clarify the details."

"Okay. You're going to move in here."

She nodded. "And just where will I be sleeping?"

One side of his mouth lifted in the sexiest grin she'd ever seen, and her stomach flip-flopped. His dark eyes bore into hers. "Wherever you want."

She immediately pictured being wrapped in Daniel's arms in a shared bed. She had no doubt making love with him would be heavenly. That was why they couldn't be intimate even once.

"Relax, Brittany," he continued. "Our marriage will be in name only, just as we agreed. You'll sleep in a guest room and I'll sleep in my room. Unless you choose for it to be otherwise. My door will always be open."

She forced her longings down. There was no way she could walk through his bedroom door. Not when one day she'd have to walk out the front door and out of his life. "I'll take the guest room."

"I thought you would. Remember, I have no expectations of a wedding night or a honeymoon. Does that put you at ease?"

She nodded. But why did she suddenly wish he wasn't so honorable? "I know our marriage will be in name only, but I won't feel comfortable with you dating anyone else."

"No problem with that."

"Really?"

"Yes. I don't want to see a different woman every night, like before. My life is different now. I have Hailey and she has to come first. I haven't dated since she's come to live with me. And I'm happy with that. I'd choose my daughter over a bunch of women any day of the week and twice on Sunday."

"Really?" She couldn't quite keep the skepticism from her voice. If he noticed, he chose to ignore it.

"Yes."

She'd expected a more detailed answer, but

one wasn't forthcoming. Instead they sat in silence as they finished their drinks, looking out the windows. She would never tire of looking at the Montana sky, especially here on the ranch where there was no light to compete with the stars. Despite the fact that she was comfortable here with him—or maybe because of it—she stood. "It's getting late. I need to get going."

He stood slowly. "If you have to."

"I do. I have to go to work in the morning." Work. Where she was going to have to announce her engagement. She knew her co-workers would be happy for her. They'd no doubt want to talk about her engagement all day. She didn't know how she would manage to fake it for the next two weeks.

They walked to the door. She turned to say goodnight as he reached for the doorknob bringing their lips within mere centimeters of touching. The heat from his body encircled her, tempting her to lean in closer. As her eyes started to drift shut, she jerked back, opened the door and darted down the stairs before she did something stupid like kiss him.

By the time she'd gotten into her car she was breathing hard. That was close. Being around Daniel was awakening desires and emotions that needed to stay dormant. She needed to get a grip on that. More than that, she needed someone she could confide in. Someone who wouldn't judge her or be disappointed in her. Amanda.

Amanda was not only her roommate. She was her best friend. Brittany knew she could tell her the truth and trust her to keep it to herself. Besides, she lived with Brittany and knew there hadn't been a whirlwind romance or a romance of any kind. Brittany might be able to fool people who didn't know she'd spent most nights at home alone, but she couldn't fool Amanda even if she wanted to. That meant she could tell Amanda the truth. And Brittany really did need to talk.

Luckily, Amanda was home when Brittany arrived.

"Hey," Amanda said.

"Hey, yourself. Got a minute?"

Amanda put down the laundry she was folding at the kitchen table. "As a matter of fact, I do."

"Good. I need a favor."

"Name it."

Brittany blew out a breath. "I need you to be my maid of honor."

Amanda laughed. "Good one. The Brittany Brandt I know is not even thinking about marriage. In fact, she's not even dating anyone seriously."

Brittany held out her left hand, revealing the gorgeous engagement ring. She still couldn't believe she was wearing it, but couldn't imagine taking it off.

Amanda's eyes grew wide and her mouth fell open. She raced over and grabbed Brittany's hand. "Is that real?"

"Yes. And no."

"Yes *and* no?"

Brittany nodded. "The sapphire and the diamonds are real. The ring is real."

"Is it …an engagement ring?"

"Yes. And the engagement is real. Sorta."

Amanda blinked a few times and put her hand to her head. "You're going to have to spell it out a little bit more for me. Like whom you're engaged to, for starters."

"Okay. But first you have to swear on all that you love to keep what I'm about to say a secret."

Amanda drew an X across her heart. "I swear on all that I love to keep what you're about to say a secret."

"Thanks."

"Now, tell me what is going on."

"You might want to sit down for this. And I know I need to."

Brittany pulled out a chair and dropped into it and Amanda did the same. Amanda stared at Brittany. "Tell me."

"Daniel Dubois asked me to marry him and I said yes."

"Excuse me, what?"

"You heard me."

"You and Daniel Dubois? The same Daniel Dubois that you called a rich guy who thought he was entitled to have whatever he wanted whenever he wanted. That Daniel Dubois?"

"That would be the one."

"And you're going to marry him. Why? Did he decide he wants you?"

"Sort of." Brittany closed her eyes for a second. "He's in a custody battle and needs a wife to improve his chances of winning."

"Custody? Of whom?"

"His daughter. Actually, she's his niece." Brittany explained about Daniel's sister's death and the lawsuit brought by Hailey's paternal grandparents. "He really loves Hailey and wants to honor his sister's wish that he raise her."

"And you've met Hailey?"

"I have. She's the sweetest little thing. Cute as a button."

"Does your family know?"

"Only about the wedding, not the reason behind it. They met Daniel and Hailey today. They liked them."

"Of course they did. Your family likes everybody."

"True."

Amanda tapped her lips with a finger but didn't say anything else.

"You're thinking about something. Go ahead and say it."

"I can see what Daniel and Hailey get out of this. He gets to raise her and she gets to stay with the person she knows. But what do you get? The way I see it, you have a lot to lose and nothing to gain."

"What am I losing?"

"Possibly your heart. I know you say you don't want kids, but I've seen you with them. You're great. What if you fall in love with Hailey and then have to say goodbye to her when this marriage ends?"

"We're not going to be married that long, so I don't have to worry about getting too attached. Not only that, Daniel and I aren't emotionally involved, so we aren't going to have a bitter breakup when we end our marriage. I'm sure he'll let me see Hailey from time to time if I want."

"And what happens if you become emotionally involved with him? What if you fall in love with Daniel Dubois?"

"That's not going to happen. He's not my type." Brittany mentally crossed her fingers, as if that childish gesture would somehow make the lie the truth. Because Daniel Dubois might not have started out as her type, but he was definitely becoming her type. The better she got to know him, the more she liked him. "And as far as not getting anything out of this, Daniel is going to give me enough money to start my own event planning business."

"That's something, I suppose."

"I can tell you aren't totally on board with this."

"I didn't say that. I admit the plan is a little crazy—well, a lot crazy—but I understand why you agreed. And it's not for the money. You've always helped anyone in need. You've never gone this far before, but it's completely in character."

"So, does that mean you'll stand up for me?"

"I guess it does. Just tell me when."

"Two weeks from now."

"Wow. That's fast."

"Yes. It can't be helped."

Amanda smiled and grabbed the ever-growing stack of bridal magazines from the table. "I guess we'd better start looking at wedding dresses for you, too."

"So, tomorrow's the big day."

Daniel turned to look at his best friend, Stephanos Dimitry. Daniel's friends had arrived last night, and they'd had dinner out. Tonight they were hanging out together at his house. It had been just like old times. The four of them had spent hours recalling the past and embellishing stories that they'd all known were exaggerations of the truth.

Daniel then glanced briefly through the glass door at Rodney and William inside. He had missed his college friends—especially Stephanos. He'd missed the time the two of them had spent working to make their company a success. They'd filled long hours together at work, building their bioengineering company, and even more hours at play, dating some of the hottest women in Texas and then jetting off to Greece, where Stephanos's father lived, for long weekends. Despite the good times, Daniel didn't regret leaving the company and moving to Montana. But having the three of them here made him realize that no matter how many new friends he made, he still needed his old ones. He vowed not to lose touch with them like he had with Jane.

Looking back at Stephanos, who'd walked outside with him onto the patio, he said, "Yes, it is." Excitement had been building over the past few days.

"It's not too late to call the whole thing off."

"Why would I do something like that?"

"Because," Stephanos pointed out, "you're treating marriage like a business deal instead of a sacred institution."

"A sacred institution?"

"You know what I mean. Marriage isn't something to be used to win a lawsuit. Or to get seed money for your business."

"I shouldn't have told you. If I had known you were going to judge me, I wouldn't have. And you haven't met Brittany yet, so don't base your opinion of her on this deal. She's marrying me to help me keep Hailey."

Only yesterday his lawyer had informed him that the Larimar's attorney had demanded custody once more. And that they were insisting on weekend visitation—at their home—as if he would ever agree to let them take Hailey anywhere. Daniel had also been informed that a social worker would be making a visit in the coming weeks. No, there would be no backing out. Everything depended on this wedding taking place as scheduled.

"And for the money you're giving her," Stephanos pointed out.

"That was my idea. She never asked for a cent."

"But she's still taking it."

"Stephanos." Daniel's voice was steely, designed to stop Stephanos in his tracks. Nobody, and that included his best friend, was going to malign Brittany in Daniel's presence.

Stephanos held up his hands in surrender. "Okay. So she's not a gold digger. My point is still valid. Marriage is special and should be treated that way."

"I know. But this is an extraordinary situation." Daniel looked at his friend. "I'm sorry for putting you in this position. I shouldn't have confided in you and asked you to keep it from Rodney and William."

"I'm your best friend." Stephanos heaved out a sigh. "I understand why you're doing this. It's not the way that I would have handled things, but I get it."

"I just can't lose Hailey."

"You won't. Now, come on back inside. We're getting ready to call it a night and head to the hotel."

"You guys know you could have stayed here. I have plenty of room."

"And a baby who needs her sleep."

Daniel followed his friend back into the house. William and Rodney stood when he entered. "Thanks again for coming, guys. I'll see you in the morning."

Daniel watched as his friends climbed into their rental car and drove away. Stephanos's words haunted him as he turned out the lights and headed upstairs. Was he doing the right thing by marrying Brittany? Or was he making a huge mistake? Whatever, it was too late to back out now. He would just say his vows tomorrow and hope for the best.

Chapter Ten

Brittany's heart was thudding so hard she wouldn't be surprised if it forced a way out of her chest. In exactly twenty minutes, she would be walking down the aisle to marry Daniel Dubois. The doubts that she'd shoved down over the past two weeks suddenly surfaced and threatened to overwhelm her.

What in the world was she doing? Why had she agreed to marry Daniel? Sure, she believed that he and Hailey belonged together, but did that mean Brittany had to marry him? It had seemed like a good idea at the time, but now that the seconds were ticking down,

Brittany's feet were beginning to feel a slight chill.

Guests were arriving. Though they'd put the wedding together rather quickly, she'd done everything in her power to make it elegant. DJ's Deluxe might not be the Ritz, but she and Reese, who was acting as her wedding coordinator, her sisters and Amanda had transformed it. They'd covered the walls with silk fabric and added pedestals wrapped with greenery and flowers. The entire place looked like a fairy-tale wedding was about to take place. In a way, it was. Not in the romantic sense where the couple would live happily ever after, but rather in the sense that nothing about it was real. It was all make-believe.

A string quintet was playing chamber music and it floated into the makeshift dressing room. Every detail had been seen to, down to the order of the musical selections. Only three more songs before the wedding would start.

Stephanie finished Brittany's makeup and Tiffany adjusted her veil.

"You look really beautiful," Tiffany said, clasping her hands against her chest. "Daniel won't be able to keep his eyes off you."

"Thank you." Brittany's voice caught in her throat. Turning to look at herself in the mirror, she couldn't believe that the glamorous reflection was her. Suddenly she felt like a bride. Though Brittany had chosen a white dress that stopped at the knee, the bodice had an elaborate lace-and-bead design. Her veil, though simple, reached the hem of her dress.

"You three look beautiful, too," Brittany said, rising from her chair. "Thanks so much for being a part of my special day." She hugged her sisters and Amanda. "I have gifts for you."

"You didn't need to do that," Amanda said. Brittany's sisters echoed the sentiment.

"Of course I did. It's tradition. More than that, you all mean so much to me." She'd found silver bracelets and earrings that would look lovely with their dresses. They'd selected elegant pink silk that fit at the waist, skimmed their hips and floated around their knees. Their silver shoes matched the color of the groomsmen's ties.

They opened their gifts, then quickly removed their earrings and put on the new jewelry.

A knock sounded on the door and her father poked his head in. "Are you ready?"

"Yes."

"Good." He stepped inside and then kissed her cheek. "You look positively radiant."

"Thanks, Dad."

"Daniel is a fine man. I know you'll be happy with him."

Brittany, Daniel and Hailey had gone to visit her parents three more times over the past two weeks. It had been Daniel's idea. He'd wanted her parents to know him better. She'd teased him that he'd only wanted to eat more of her mother's cooking, but inside Brittany had been pleased. Though their marriage was a sham, Daniel had behaved like a real fiancé, which had put her parents at ease. Unfortunately, it had had the opposite effect on her.

Reese stepped inside. "It's time to start."

Brittany's breath caught in her throat. She might be entering into a marriage of convenience, but it was still a marriage. *Her* marriage. It might not be a permanent union, but she was going to do her best to make Daniel happy.

Brittany and her bridesmaids filed into the back of the dining room. A curtain hung from the ceiling, so they were out of sight of the guests. The chairs had been arranged in two sections with a wide aisle down the center. Though they'd planned to have a small wedding with only immediate family, the guest list had ballooned to seventy-five, which included their closest friends as well as the Bronco elite.

Her cousin's three-year-old twins, Leo and Natalia, were serving as ring bearer and flower girl. Leo kept checking himself out in his tiny tuxedo and grinning. Natalia spun in a circle, making the skirt on her pink dress fly into the air.

All at once the quiet talk stopped and the

quintet began to play the song Brittany had selected for the entrance of the bridal party. Tiffany walked down the aisle beside Rodney, followed by Stephanie and William. Amanda walked down next, followed by Leo and Natalia.

And then it was time for Brittany and her father to enter. As she took his arm, she began to tremble. He covered her hand with his and gave it a gentle squeeze. She glanced up and saw Daniel standing at the end of the aisle. Dressed in a perfectly tailored black tuxedo that emphasized his broad shoulders and trim waist, he looked like every dream she'd ever had come to life. His eyes were riveted to her as if he'd never seen her before. He smiled and she smiled in return. Just looking at him soothed her. What had she been so worried about? This was *Daniel*.

She and her father had reached the middle of the aisle when Daniel took a step in her direction. And then another one. What was he doing? He was supposed to wait by the floral arch, beside his best man, until she reached him. But he kept walking and didn't stop until he stood in front of her.

"I'll take it from here," he said to her father.

"All right now," one of her cousins called out. "Go get your woman."

Several people laughed and a murmur filled the room. Brittany was so focused on Daniel that she couldn't make out the words.

Her father kissed her cheek and then relinquished his hold on her. Daniel held out his elbow and she wrapped her arm around his. Smiling, they walked to the front of the room and stood before her pastor. The room and everyone in it faded away as she became acutely aware of the man beside her. The man she was about to join her life to.

"Dearly Beloved," Pastor King intoned, his baritone voice filling the room, "we are gathered here today to join this man and this woman in holy matrimony."

Brittany had heard the familiar words many times in her life, yet now they took on new meaning. This time she wasn't witnessing two other people become husband and wife.

This was her wedding. Daniel was about to become her husband and she was about to become his wife. This was real.

Before long they reached the place in the ceremony where they were to exchange vows. Though Daniel had been indifferent to most of the choices, he'd wanted to write his own vows. Initially, Brittany hadn't understood his reasoning. Then it occurred to her that he hadn't wanted to vow to love, honor and cherish her. The thought had pinched her heart a little, but she'd forced the pain away. Why should he say words he didn't mean?

Maybe he was onto something. She didn't want to swear before God and everyone that she would love Daniel forever, so she'd come up with her own vows, too. They hadn't shared what they'd written, so they'd each be hearing the words for the first time now.

Daniel took her hand and looked into her eyes. His voice was firm and steady. "Brittany. You came into my life when I least expected it. Your heart is so pure. So beautiful. You're a treasure I know I don't deserve. I'll do everything in my power to be worthy of you. I can't promise to never make a mistake, because I know I will. But I can promise to learn from them and to do better. Of all the good things in my life, you are far and away the best. Thank you for giving me a chance to experience real love."

Brittany's vision blurred as she listened to Daniel's words. He sounded so sincere she could almost believe that he was in love with her. Though she didn't need a man in her life to complete her, she suddenly wished this was real and that they really were joining their lives and becoming one.

But this was playacting. He'd said his part. Now it was time to deliver her lines.

When she'd written her vows, she'd tried to imagine how a bride who was marrying the love of her life would feel. The words she would use to convey those emotions… After listening to Daniel, her vows suddenly seemed inadequate, but they were all she had.

"Daniel." Her voice was a trembling whisper, so she cleared her throat and started over.

"Daniel. I had my entire life mapped out before I met you. I knew where I was going and when I would get there. And then we met. Suddenly my life took a turn along a different path. I'm not certain where the road will lead, but as long as you're by my side, I'm eager to discover what awaits us."

When she finished reciting her vow, she was as breathless as if she'd just run a mile. Reminding herself that none of this was real only worked for so long. She heard people murmuring about true love, and how romantic their vows had been, and she felt a twinge of guilt. That feeling grew as they lit the unity candle, signifying their eternal love for each other, but there was no turning back now.

It was finally time to jump the broom, signaling the end of the ceremony. Tiffany and Stephanie hadn't decorated any old broom, but rather had created one from a branch they'd found in a park near their home. They'd tied ribbons and flowers on it, making it a one-of-a-kind work of art. One of the ushers carried it into the room and handed it to Pastor King.

The pastor turned and spoke to the guests. "In the tradition of our ancestors, the bride and groom will now jump the broom. This symbolizes crossing the threshold into the land of matrimony. It marks the beginning of a new life, sweeping aside the old, and welcoming a new beginning."

When the broom was set before Brittany and Daniel, they joined hands. Then, looking at each other, they hopped over the broom.

"You may salute your bride," Pastor King said.

Brittany had thought about this moment from the time she'd agreed to marry Daniel. Somehow, in all of her imagining, she hadn't gotten the emotion right. As she stared into his dark brown eyes, all thought fled, leaving only one sincere feeling behind. *Desire.* More than anything, she wanted to feel Daniel's lips pressing against hers.

Her longing must have showed on her face because his eyes flashed for a moment before he lowered his head, bringing his lips into contact with hers. Electricity shot through her body and her knees buckled. Instantly his arms were around her waist, supporting her. Of their own volition, her arms encircled his neck and she moved more closely to him, deepening the kiss. Feelings she'd never experienced—didn't know she could experience—flooded her body and she didn't want the moment to end.

Daniel began to ease away and she moaned in protest. She felt him smile against her mouth and her senses returned. They were in front of their nearest and dearest and she was behaving as if she was a sixteen-year-old in the back seat of her boyfriend's car. She and Daniel eased away from each other and the roaring in her ears was replaced by the cheers of the crowd.

"Ladies and gentlemen, I present for the first time anywhere, Mr. and Mrs. Daniel Dubois," Pastor King said.

While everyone clapped, Brittany did her level best to regain control of herself. Daniel grabbed her hand and winked at her. He was cool as a cucumber. Apparently, the kiss was one-sided, only scorching her lips and all but roasting her insides. Fortunately, there was no time to brood about her embarrassment. That would have to wait until after the reception was over and the well-wishers had gone home. Now there were pictures to pose for and hugs and congratulations to accept.

Reese whisked the bridal party outside to pose for pictures in the glorious, sunny day. Meanwhile waiters served the guests from trays of appetizers and beverages.

"Smile," the photographer said, pulling Brittany's attention to the here-and-now and away from what was going on inside the restaurant. As they posed for one picture after another, she couldn't help but wonder what the photographs would reveal. Would her inner turmoil show on her face? Would her unexpected desire be revealed in her eyes? Whatever the case, she silently vowed to hide the wedding album forever.

Thirty minutes and hundreds of pictures

later, the wedding party went back inside the restaurant. The altar had been replaced by a gorgeously decorated table where Daniel, Brittany and their attendants would sit.

Daniel led her through the maze of tables, greeting their friends and family with an ease that Brittany envied. She was still trying to get a handle on her renegade feelings and could barely manage to smile.

As they reached their table, DJ Traub, the owner of the restaurant, approached them to offer his congratulations.

"Thanks for letting us have the restaurant on such short notice," Daniel said.

DJ smiled. "Your wife is very persuasive and very hard to say no to."

"I know." Daniel gave Brittany a sexy smile that had her toes curling. "I don't think I'll be able to say no to her for at least a hundred years."

"It really is my pleasure to host your wedding and reception. We'll start serving in about fifteen minutes. Is that okay with you?"

Daniel and Brittany exchanged a look. Daniel nodded. "That's fine."

Brittany was able to see all of their guests from her chair. Her parents were seated nearby. Although this was an adults-only affair, Hailey had been included. They'd requested and received a high chair for her, but she was currently seated on Mallory's lap, contentedly playing with a stuffed horse. Brittany had no doubt that if Hailey became fussy, one of her brothers would entertain her. Lucas and Ethan were currently locked in a battle to become her favorite uncle.

Reese stood in the back, conferring with the new restaurant manager. Brittany wondered if there was a problem. The marriage might not be real, but she still wanted the reception to go off without a hitch.

"Relax," Daniel said, leaning close and whispering into her ear. The warmth from his body caressed her bare shoulders, making her shiver. How could he expect her to relax when his nearness awakened everything feminine inside her? Did he think she could be calm when being close to him made her nerves jangle like wind chimes in a tornado? Of course, she couldn't say that. He was clearly unaffected by her and she needed to find a way to become just as indifferent to him. Until that time arrived, she'd have to fake it.

She couldn't let him know that this whole wedding and the kiss was wreaking havoc with her common sense. Not when, to him, this was simply a part of doing whatever it took to keep Hailey. Brittany did have her pride. She told herself that the feelings she was currently experiencing weren't real. It just turned out that she was a method actor. Pretending to be a besotted bride had turned her into one. Once this was over, she'd go back to being Brittany Brandt—er, Brittany Dubois, calm, cool and collected.

"I'm trying to relax," she told him. "I guess it's the event planner in me."

"But you hired your friend to do that. And she's doing a magnificent job. This room looks like one of the ballrooms in the fairy tales that I read to Hailey."

Brittany looked around. "It really does look magnificent, doesn't it?

"Yes. So smile and enjoy your dinner."

Brittany bared her teeth and Daniel laughed at the face she'd made. "You are so silly, Brittany."

She smiled for real this time, amazed that he'd managed to ease her worry.

Brittany enjoyed every course of the delicious food. She'd worked with DJ to create a special menu for this occasion. Though the restaurant didn't ordinarily serve red wine braised short rib and pan seared salmon, they'd managed to prepare it to her satisfaction.

Suddenly, Brittany became aware of a tinkling sound that clashed with the soft music. When she recognized it as silverware clicking against the crystal glasses, the universal signal guests gave when they wanted the happy couple to kiss, anticipation mingled with dread.

This time she was determined not to make a fool of herself. And she definitely wasn't going to go overboard as if she and Daniel were engaged in a make-out session. Smiling, she leaned over and pecked him on the lips. The guests groaned in protest.

"Surely we can do better than that," Daniel said.

Before she could respond, his lips were on hers in a searing kiss. It only lasted a few seconds, but during that brief time, the earth moved, shifting on its axis. Her heart fluttered and jumped around her chest before settling in its original place.

"I told you we could do better," Daniel said before picking up his fork and turning his attention to his baked potato. Brittany, on the other hand, tried to douse the flame of desire raging inside her by downing her glass of ice water.

Once the meal was finished, the wedding cake, wheeled out on a small table, was set in front of Daniel and Brittany. Grabbing the decorative knife in their hands, they sliced into the cake then set the piece onto a crystal plate. They each picked up a portion and, interlocking their arms, fed each other.

Brittany had never done anything so intimate, much less with an audience, and her hand trembled as it brushed against Daniel's bottom lip. His tongue darted out and touched her finger and she sucked in a breath. He had to know what he was doing to her. But then again, he was playing a role. After all, he had the most to lose if they failed, so he had to give an Academy Award-winning performance of a happy groom. Brittany had no idea how the court case would play out, so it was possible that any of the people in this room could be questioned about their marriage. After watching Daniel's act, the guests would be able to say that she and Daniel may have had a whirlwind courtship, but their relationship was authentic.

After the ever-present photographer snapped even more pictures, the cake was returned to the kitchen where it would be cut and served to the guests.

Amanda approached them. She smiled at Daniel and then hugged Brittany. "Everything is so beautiful. I hope Holt's and my wedding is as perfect as this."

Daniel caressed Brittany's cheek. "I'm going to check on Hailey. I'll meet you back at the table in a few?"

Brittany nodded.

After he left, she turned to Amanda, who suddenly looked sad. Her smile had faded and the light in her eyes had dimmed. "What?" Brittany asked.

"Nothing. At least, nothing I can talk about in a room filled with your wedding guests."

"Come on. If you can't talk to your best friend, who can you talk to?" Brittany led Amanda to a secluded area of the restaurant. "Talk to me."

"It's just that this wedding is so beautiful. And everyone is so happy."

"So why would that make you unhappy?"

"I was thinking about Winona Cobbs and Josiah Abernathy and their long-lost baby, Beatrix. They never had the chance to be a happy family. Josiah has dementia now and rarely speaks so it was a big deal when he said he wanted someone to find his baby. And from what I understand, Winona isn't doing too well physically. Beatrix would be in her seventies now, so she might not even be alive."

Amanda had been using her social media skills to help their friend Melanie and her fiancé Gabe Abernathy try to locate Beatrix. "I thought that you'd gotten a response to your query. You were so excited that you might have found Josiah and Winona's child."

Amanda's shoulders slumped.

"Well, it turns out that Bernadette Jefferson wasn't Beatrix, after all."

"Oh. How disappointing." Amanda was really invested in finding Beatrix.

"Infuriating is more like it. Bernadette was a fraud. She knew she wasn't Beatrix. She was just an imposter hoping to shake down the Abernathy family for money."

"That's awful."

"Yes. Frauds and liars are the lowest of the low."

Brittany winced.

"I didn't mean you. You aren't a fraud or a liar."

"I'm pretending to be a bride," she whispered.

"You are a bride. And you're married to Daniel Dubois. That's the truth."

"You know what I mean. We aren't in love." She was tempted to shield her mouth when she spoke but refrained.

"Maybe not. Yet."

"What do you mean *yet*?"

"There were some serious sparks flying between the two of you. And that kiss?" Amanda waved her hand in front of her face. "There was so much steam, I'm surprised your hair is still curled."

Brittany's face grew hot and she looked around to be sure they weren't overheard. Nobody was near and they were not attracting unusual attention. "You're imagining things."

"Remember. I'm the one who told you there

was something between you and Daniel before any of this occurred. You denied it rather quickly, so I let it go. Maybe I was right all along."

Brittany didn't reply, but inside she hoped Amanda was wrong. The last thing she wanted to do was to fall in love with her temporary husband. Especially since said husband gave no indication that he was falling for her.

"Anyway," Amanda continued, "given your insistence that marriage was the last thing on your mind, I think it's pretty ironic that you've gotten married before me."

"That's one word for it. Have you set a date yet?"

Amanda shook her head. "Still planning for the fall. When we have an exact date, you'll be the first to know."

Brittany was about to reply when she heard a ruckus. Off to the side and away from other guests, she saw Daphne Taylor and her father, Cornelius, arguing—most likely about the animal shelter. Again. Brittany didn't understand how a family could be at odds with each other like the Taylors. Though she and her parents occasionally disagreed, they didn't fight. She'd always believed other families were the same. Looking at the way Daphne and Cornelius were going at it, Brittany realized how wrong she'd been.

She couldn't let them continue to argue without intervening. Daphne was a friend of hers. Not only that, this was Brittany's wedding reception. She didn't want a scene. "I'll talk to you later."

"Want me to go with you?" Amanda asked.

"No. I'm sure they won't appreciate an audience."

Amanda nodded then walked away.

Brittany approached father and daughter, who were so engrossed in their heated discussion that they didn't notice her.

"Is everything okay?' Brittany asked in her sweetest voice.

"Fine," Daphne said, her jaw clenched. "I'm glad I ran into you. I want to extend my heartfelt congratulations, but I won't be staying."

"Oh, don't go. The dancing is going to begin soon. We've hired a great DJ and it's going to be a lot of fun."

"I'm sure it will, but I need to go." Daphne gave Brittany a quick hug then, without giving her father a second look, turned and stalked away.

Sighing, Brittany turned to Cornelius. She didn't want to get in the middle of a family fight, but she wondered why he'd let Daphne walk out when she was so obviously upset. Brittany knew her own father would never do that.

"Will you be staying?" Brittany asked Cornelius.

"Are you asking me to leave?"

"Not at all," Brittany replied smoothly. Asking him to leave would be ungracious. Besides, she was still hoping to land the Taylor account. "As I told Daphne, the party is about to get started. Shall we return to the reception?"

He looked at her with keen eyes then held out his arm to her. "Absolutely."

As they returned to the reception, Brittany's heart ached for her friend and she wondered why Cornelius couldn't have treated Daphne as graciously as he was treating her.

Chapter Eleven

Daniel glanced at Brittany and his heartrate sped up. As the day had progressed, his attraction to her had grown and he'd felt the buzz of excitement each time they'd touched. The first dance had just been announced and now he was about to hold her in his arms again. The very thought made his blood pulse through his veins.

Every head was turned to the dance floor. Brittany stood a few feet away, a shy smile on her face. He knew from spending time with her that she was uncomfortable being the center of attention. He could also tell from the way she nibbled on her bottom lip that the deception was weighing on her. If he could take away her discomfort, he would.

Though she didn't know it, the way her tongue swept across her lip turned him on. Truth be told, everything about Brittany was starting to turn him on. She looked both sweet and sexy in her wedding dress that revealed the shapeliest legs he'd ever seen. They looked even more enticing in her three-inch strappy white shoes.

She'd removed her veil and had freed her hair from the fancy twist it had been styled in. Now her hair floated around her bare shoulders, her curls bouncing whenever she turned her head.

Taking her hand, he led her to the dance floor then pulled her close. She held her body a little stiffly as if unsure of herself. Her sweet scent encircled him, and he closed his eyes in utter bliss.

They'd spent many hours trying to choose the song for their first dance, debating and laughing at each other's choices. It hadn't taken long for them to realize that none of the songs fit their situation. In fact, the song that could adequately sum up their relationship hadn't yet been written. They'd narrowed the choices down to two—with him and Brittany stubbornly sticking to their favorite—and had rock, paper, scissored it. "Always and Forever," a song that had been sung at weddings for a generation or two, was the winner.

As the song played, the lyrics hit Daniel in the solar plexus. The sighs of the female guests were audible, but it was Brittany's sigh that had his heart speeding up. He'd give anything to know what she felt at this very moment.

Did she have any idea just how sexy she was or how desirable he found her? This may be a show wedding, but that didn't make him immune to her. Kissing her had aroused feelings in him that he hadn't expected. And not simply desire. He'd kissed many women in his lifetime, many of them women he'd cared a great deal for, but the reaction he'd had kissing Brittany's lips made the others pale in comparison. Truthfully, there was no comparison. These kisses—like Brittany herself—were in a category of their own.

They'd almost felt like love. But that was crazy. He wasn't in love with Brittany. He couldn't be.

As they danced across the floor, he began to wish he hadn't promised her that their relationship wouldn't be physical. Logically a marriage in name only was the best way to handle this situation. This was a business arrangement. He'd been around long enough to know that business and pleasure didn't mix. Not successfully anyway.

It was imperative that this marriage be successful. So, as he'd done earlier when he'd found himself longing to kiss her deeply, he resisted the urge and thought about something mundane, like his horses' feeding schedule.

The last note of the music faded out and he reluctantly stepped back, keeping contact with Brittany as long as he could. The DJ announced the father and daughter dance, so he relinquished Brittany to her father then went to stand against the wall where he would be able to watch them.

Stephanos came and stood beside Daniel. "I think I might have made a mistake."

"About what?"

"You. Brittany. This marriage. I think there's more between the two of you than you let on."

Daniel looked around before replying. Every eye was focused on the dance floor where Phillip swung Brittany in a waltz. Brittany had told Daniel that when she'd been a teenager, she'd loved watching couples waltz in old movies and she'd convinced her father to teach her the dance. Hopefully, he and Hailey would have a special dance of their own one day.

"You're imagining things."

"Am I?"

"Yes." Daniel shoved his hands in his pants' pockets. "Sure, I like her. What's not to like? But that's as far as my feelings are allowed to go."

"Allowed?"

"The last thing either of us needs is complications." Like kisses that made him feel more than he should.

"True," Stephanos agreed. "But sometimes you don't get what you need. Sometimes you get what you get."

"You're a philosopher now?"

Stephanos laughed and, after a moment, Daniel joined him. It didn't take a philosopher to recognize the truth in those words. That's why it was important to take the hand you were dealt and play the cards the best you could.

Daniel heard footsteps and turned around as Rodney and William joined them. "Why are you guys lurking in the corner? Don't tell me you're in the doghouse already," Rodney joked.

"Even Daniel can't get in trouble at his own wedding reception," William replied, saving Daniel the trouble.

"Speaking of getting into trouble, Brittany has some gorgeous sisters," Rodney said.

"Who are now my sisters-in-law, which

makes them off-limits." Rodney was a good guy, but he was a notorious womanizer who didn't remain with one woman for long. Given that Daniel's track record had been similar, he wasn't in a position to judge. But he wouldn't leave Stephanie or Tiffany vulnerable to a guy like Rodney, either.

"All I said was how pretty they are. I'm not planning on seducing either of them—unless I'm asked."

"Don't make me hurt you."

Rodney and William laughed. Daniel noticed that Stephanos didn't join in. There wasn't time for Daniel to ponder his friend's reaction because it was time for the bridal party to dance.

The first time he and Brittany had danced together, she'd seemed almost nervous and unsure. This time, she seemed to be enjoying it. That was good since dancing with his new wife was his new favorite thing. When the song ended, the emcee announced that the floor was open to anyone who wanted to dance.

After a few line dances and the throwing of the bouquet, Daniel noticed a marked difference in Brittany. Now that everything on the reception list had been checked off, she relaxed and truly enjoy herself. She laughed as she danced, enchanting everyone, especially him.

"I need a break," she said after a while.

"Sure." He led her back to their chairs. A passing waiter gave them drinks and, after a few sips, she smiled.

"I needed that."

"I saw you and Cornelius Taylor talking earlier. Does that mean he's going to go along with your Denim and Diamonds fundraiser idea?"

"I hope so. I guess only time will tell."

"He'd be a fool to tell you no."

She leaned over and kissed his cheek. "Thank you. That means the world to me."

His heart skipped a beat as her lips brushed his skin. He wanted another kiss. A real kiss. But that kind of thinking would only get him in trouble.

He'd nearly blown it earlier at the ceremony. Holding her soft body against his had been torture, but kissing her had nearly been his undoing. As much as he craved another taste of her, he had to keep his distance.

After she'd agreed to marry him, they'd covered every topic of their marriage and discussed it to death. They'd thought it prudent to limit their closeness. Heck, just about all of their conversations had involved ways of keeping their distance. Starting with living together. They'd been proud of their extensive planning, which left nothing to chance.

Brittany would move into the bedroom adjoining his master bath, although she'd keep her clothes in his closet to maintain the illusion that they were sharing a bed. None of his household staff lived in the main house, so that was a bonus. Not that either of them expected anyone to go snooping. But Marta wasn't blind, either. Brittany had assured him that she'd make her own bed and clean her room so Marta would never know anyone was occupying it. They'd discussed their upcoming cohabitation ad nauseam, leaving no detail uncovered.

But all that planning hadn't been as comprehensive as either of them had believed. If it had, one of them would have brought up the need to practice touching. And kissing. Had they done so, Daniel would have been prepared for the surge of electricity that shot through his body every time he brushed against her. Or breathed in her sweet scent.

And when he'd kissed her? It was as if a sign with the word *Wow* had blinked in flashing lights over his head. It was all he could do to keep a goofy grin off his face. He wasn't sure if Brittany felt the same sensation, so he'd played it cool. The last thing he wanted was for her to worry that he'd pounce on her the first chance he got. She was his wife in name only. That's all she'd agreed to. Though he might want to renegotiate a clause in their contract to include kissing, he wouldn't mention it. He couldn't risk that she'd get upset and call it quits. He'd have to stick to the original plan and figure out how to keep his body under control.

"Ready for another dance?" she asked and smiled at him.

"Absolutely."

The DJ played another slow song and he held her in his arms. He'd concentrate on controlling his body later. Right now he was going to enjoy the moment.

Brittany dropped back into her chair. She'd been dancing for half an hour, having a great time. She'd danced with just about every man in attendance. When she'd danced with Brandon and Jordan Taylor, she'd casually mentioned the relationship between their sister, Daphne, and their father. She hoped they'd speak with Cornelius and try to smooth things over with him on their sister's behalf.

Daniel presented her with a glass of champagne then sat beside her. Clinking her glass against his in a silent toast, she lifted it to her mouth and took a sip. She wasn't much of a champagne drinker, but she had to admit this stuff was good.

Daniel looked past her and she turned around. Her mother was carrying a sleeping Hailey in her arms. Her father was right behind, the strap of the diaper bag slung over his shoulder.

"We're about to leave. We just wanted to say good-night," Mallory said.

Daniel stood. "Are you sure about letting Hailey spend the night? We don't mind taking her home with us."

"Nonsense. It's your wedding night," her mother protested. "And she's become comfortable with us."

"But—"

"No buts. She'll be fine. I understand that you two don't want to take a honeymoon trip right now with Hailey being so young, but you need at least one night together as husband and wife. Consider this a wedding present."

Brittany put a hand on Daniel's arm. She knew how protective he was of Hailey. But even so, it would look really strange if he didn't want to spend his wedding night alone with his new bride. Leaning her head against his shoulder, she smiled up at him. "Mom is right. Hailey will be fine. After all the excitement, she'll probably sleep straight through the night."

Daniel smiled at her and then at her parents. "You're right. I'm being overprotective. Thanks for caring for her tonight."

Brittany was still leaning against Daniel after her parents left, and she didn't feel the need to move. He wrapped an arm around her waist, clearly comfortable with her nearness.

"You know, I guess we should be leaving soon, too," Daniel said. "It might look a little bit strange if we hang around all night."

"True. I'll let Reese know, so she can pass out the birdseed for people to toss at us."

Five minutes later, a laughing Brittany and Daniel ran from the restaurant and hopped into his Mercedes SUV. Brittany waved at the crowd, who watched them leave. She and Daniel had reserved the restaurant for the entire night, so their guests could party until the wee hours of the morning if they so desired. But for them, the party was over.

As they drove out of Bronco and toward Daniel's horse ranch, the reality of what they'd just done slammed into her. They'd really done it. They'd gotten married. For better or for worse, she was now Mrs. Daniel Dubois.

Chapter Twelve

As Daniel drove down the highway to the ranch, Brittany's breath caught in her throat and she forced herself to exhale. This was ridiculous. There was no reason for her to feel jittery. But still, her stomach was filled with butterflies crashing into each other. Her heart pounded and the blood raced through her veins.

Her wedding night was about to start.

Daniel had made it clear that he was willing to change the terms of their agreement. All she had to do was say the word. And right now, sitting beside him in his SUV, inhaling his intoxicating scent with every breath, re-negotiation held a certain appeal. She'd love to be wrapped in his strong arms, pressed against his hard chest. But she couldn't give in to the desire to have a real wedding night. Not when she knew the marriage would end as abruptly as it had begun. No, she would stick to the agreed upon terms. This was a marriage in name only.

Daniel pulled into the driveway and parked. Brittany reached to open her door, but he put a hand on her wrist, stopping her. She looked at him.

"I can do that."

"So can I."

"Humor me."

She nodded. Resisting when he was being kind would only raise questions she did not want to answer. How could she explain that she didn't want him to be charming and chivalrous? That his being so gallant gave her ideas about their relationship? She didn't want him to turn into the man that she would have dreamed of—if she'd ever dreamed of a man.

He circled the SUV, opened her door and then offered his hand. She didn't want to appear churlish, so she placed her hand in his and let him help her. Instead of releasing her hand, he tightened his grip and rubbed his thumb over her knuckles as they walked across the cobblestones. He unlocked the door and pushed it open. Before she could step inside, he swung her into his strong arms.

She gasped and her lungs were filled with his heady masculine scent. "What are you doing?"

"I have to carry you over the threshold. It's good luck."

She knew she should protest, but being in his arms felt too good. Just this once, she'd allow herself the pleasure. "I didn't know you were the superstitious type."

"I prefer to think of myself as traditional."

He stepped over the threshold and then kicked the door closed behind them. Instead of setting her on her feet, he carried her into the front room and set her on the sofa. A bottle of wine and a tray of cheese, fruit, fine chocolate and crackers was centered on the coffee table. Vases of pink roses covered every table. It was all very romantic.

"Wow," Brittany exclaimed, looking around. "This is beautiful."

"Yes."

She looked at him. "Did you do this?"

He smiled. "With a little help."

Why would he do something like this? Surely he hadn't forgotten his promise of no wedding night. Given he'd behaved honorably since they'd met, she decided not to jump to conclusions.

He shrugged out of his tuxedo jacket, loosened his tie, unfastened his diamond-stud cuff links and then rolled his shirtsleeves over twice. "Would you care for anything? A strawberry? Truffle? Or, if you're really hungry, there's food in the kitchen. We'll have to cook it since everyone is gone, but I bet neither of us had much chance to eat at the party."

They were alone? Had he sent all the staff home deliberately? Brittany's nerves went into overdrive. She and Daniel had never been alone here before. Even when his employees had gone home for the night, Hailey had still provided a buffer. Her pulse picked up.

Start as You Intend to Continue had always been Brittany's motto. If she acted nervous now, she would no doubt be nervous for the remainder of her marriage. Undoubtedly, that would make Daniel uncomfortable. They didn't need to walk on eggshells for the next few months. Besides, they'd gotten along well for the past couple of weeks. She took a deep breath and forced herself to answer calmly. "This is good for now, but I might want something else later."

"Fair enough."

They each served themselves then leaned back against the sofa. For a moment, neither of them spoke, choosing instead to feast on the fruit and cheese.

"That went well, don't you think?" Daniel asked.

"Are you kidding? We were outstanding.

No one suspected a thing. You definitely have a career in theater if this ranch thing doesn't pan out."

He laughed. "You weren't so shabby yourself. Everyone totally believes you're madly in love with me. But then, what's not to love?"

She threw a grape at him. He caught it and popped it into his mouth.

Brittany picked up a square of chocolate. She needed to distract herself from her attraction to him so she changed the subject. "Have you heard from your attorney lately?"

Daniel's smile faded and she wished she could take back the question and just enjoy the moment. "Yes. He said we can expect to hear from a court-appointed social worker who'll be interviewing us as well as the Larimars. Then the social worker will make a recommendation to the court about who should get custody of Hailey. The judge isn't bound by that recommendation, although my attorney says judges generally do what the social worker thinks is best."

"One more person to deceive."

"We aren't deceiving anyone. We're legally married. The details of our marriage aren't anyone else's business. Do you actually believe that every couple acts the same at home as they do in public? Do you think they don't have secrets? Theirs might be different from ours, but believe me, they exist."

"But they're in love."

"How do you know that?" He laughed. "Haven't you heard of staying together for the kids? Or the money? Heck there's that old seventies' song—'It's Cheaper to Keep Her.'"

Brittany laughed as she knew he'd intended. "You're right. Thank you for reminding me of that. And regardless of how wonderful Hailey's paternal grandparents may be, they can't possibly be better for Hailey than you are."

She'd obviously said the right thing because he smiled. "Thanks for that."

They sat for a while, letting the peace of the quiet night wash over them. Finally, Brittany stood, plate in hand. "I don't know about you, but I'm beat. I think I'll head on up to bed. These past couple of days have been exhausting."

"Okay." Daniel stood and took her plate. "I'll take care of cleaning this up. I'll probably stay down here for a while and watch a little TV."

"I guess I'll say good-night, then."

He kissed her cheek. "Good night."

Brittany managed to act as if his kiss hadn't turned her knees to mush. She felt Daniel's eyes on her as she walked up the stairs, but she didn't turn around to look at him. Feeling as confused as she was, there was no guarantee that she wouldn't go running back for a second kiss. Or a third. When she reached the second floor, she turned and walked down the hallway to her bedroom.

Daniel had showed her the room and explained that the architect who'd designed the house had been enamored of the idea of the master and mistress of the house having their own private bedrooms with a shared master bath in between. Since Daniel had liked the plans, he'd gone along with it. She wondered what he thought of the design now.

Daniel had given her the option of sleeping in any of the other guest rooms, but she'd thought this one would work best. It might have raised red flags if she'd used another bathroom. The social worker might interview the staff. Brittany didn't want the maid to mention damp towels in a guest bathroom that might bring the status of her and Daniel's marriage into question.

Brittany stepped into the room and dropped onto the bed. The mattress was so soft, like sinking into a cloud. She just sat there awhile, letting the enormity of the day slide from her shoulders. Then she took off her dress and headed for the bathroom. What she needed was a good soak in Daniel's gigantic jetted tub.

She spotted a container of bubbling bath salts and gave thanks for whoever had bought them. Deciding she'd rather have the scent and bubbles over jets, she tossed a handful into the tub then turned on the water. While the tub filled, she washed off her makeup. She didn't see a shower cap, so she pinned her hair on top of her head. When the tub was full, she finished undressing and sank into the fragrant water.

Closing her eyes, she saw the images of the day flash in front of her. The sights and sounds of her wedding. The feel of Daniel's arms wrapped around her. Her skin began to tingle as she recalled just how good Daniel's kiss felt. It was almost like being in love, which didn't make a lick of sense.

Brittany didn't believe in love at first sight or anything remotely close to it. Love was something that grew over time. A lot of time. It came from shared experiences and shared values. She and Daniel hadn't done many things together—they hadn't known each other long enough. And it was way too soon to know if they had the same values.

Of course, none of that mattered when it came to animal attraction. Without question, she was attracted to Daniel. How could she not be? He was six feet of male excellence.

His muscular body was well proportioned and the result of hard work, not steroids. He was clean-shaved, so none of his gorgeous face was covered by hair—not that a beard or mustache could mask his good looks. Nothing could do that.

His eyes revealed the sharp mind and quick wit he possessed. Though he was occasionally impatient, he had a kind heart. Especially where Hailey was concerned. If he was occasionally abrupt, it was because he was worried about something, not because he was inconsiderate. Once she'd figured that out, she'd been more inclined to give him a little bit of grace.

While she'd been soaking, the water had cooled, and she was getting cold. She hadn't been making excuses when she'd told Daniel she was sleepy. She was beat. Climbing out of the tub, she grabbed a plush bath towel, dried off and then wrapped the towel around her body.

Since her clothes were in Daniel's bedroom, she twisted the doorknob leading to his room.

She'd get a nightgown and the clothes she intended to wear tomorrow and scoot into her room while he was downstairs watching TV. She opened the door, took one step and bumped into his bare chest.

Gasping, she jumped back into the bathroom. "What are you doing in there?"

"It's my bedroom. Remember? What are you doing coming in here?" He raised an eyebrow. "I thought we'd ironed out the details of our marriage and sleeping arrangements."

"I thought you were downstairs."

"I was. But the program I was watching ended and there was nothing else on that I wanted to see. You came up here over an hour ago, so I figured you were asleep by now."

"I was taking a bath," she said unnecessarily. She was standing there in nothing but a towel for goodness' sake. She tucked the end more firmly between her breasts. The last thing she wanted was for it to fall off. As it was, very little was left to Daniel's imagination.

And speaking of leaving nothing to the

imagination. Daniel was dressed only in his tuxedo pants. The brown skin of his muscular chest looked so good she had to ball her hands into fists to keep from touching it. But that didn't keep her mind from thinking of how good it would feel to caress the muscles of his six-pack abs.

"I can come back later," he offered, turning to go.

"Wait." She grabbed his arm and the heat of his skin nearly burned her hand. She yanked her hand away and took two steps farther into the bathroom. The sensation was so strong, it took a minute for her mind to clear.

"Wait for what?" Daniel asked when she just stood there, her mouth hanging open.

"I'm finished in here. I was going to your room to get a nightgown. I'll get one and you can take your shower."

He leaned against the door frame, effectively blocking her way. "I didn't think this through. This whole clothes thing is going to be inconvenient for you."

"It's not that bad."

He smiled. "You know, you have to be the most positive person I've ever met."

Were they just going to stand there half-naked and talk? Apparently so. "Why wouldn't I be positive? It's not as if this is something that just happened to me. I made a decision that comes with consequences. When I agreed to marry you, my eyes were wide open. Besides, this has to be more inconvenient for you than it is for me."

"How do you figure that?"

"This is your house. You're used to doing everything your way. This is your bathroom, but you suddenly have to share it with me. Same as your closet. You'll have to get used to having me around all the time now that I won't be going home at the end of the night."

"That won't be a hardship. In a house this size, we won't have to see each other unless we want to." He gave her a devilish smile. "And if you're going to wander about wearing nothing but a tiny towel, I can guarantee I won't complain."

She poked him in his chest. "Sure, if you promise to never wear a shirt."

His eyes widened and he laughed. Clearly, she'd surprised him. "You might be on to something."

She grabbed a hold of herself. What was she doing? She couldn't flirt with him. "No, I'm not. Step aside, so I can get my night-gown."

He stepped back and she walked around him and into the master bedroom. Brittany's eyes were automatically drawn to the king bed in front of a wall of windows. The curtains were still open, revealing an Olympic-size swimming pool and patio. But it wasn't the view that held her attention. It was the flower petals scattered across the floor from the door to the bed that had her riveted in place.

She heard the rumble of his deep voice behind her. "I didn't tell Marta to do that. She must have thought it would make the room more romantic for our wedding night."

Brittany couldn't decide if she felt more

disappointed or relieved to know the petals hadn't been his idea. "It was nice of her."

"Yes."

"I'll be certain to mention how much I liked it."

"Good thinking."

"What time does your staff usually arrive?" she asked.

"About seven. Why?"

"So I know what time I have to be up and have the bed made each morning. We can't afford slipups."

"If you want, you can always get into my bed," he suggested, making her heart skip a beat.

"I thought we had a deal. No funny business."

"That's not what I meant. It just didn't come out right. I get up early, so if you want to sleep in, feel free to hop into my bed when I get out."

Just like that, Brittany's mind went there. She could imagine lying in Daniel's bed, still warm from his body, her head on the pillow where his head had been only moments earlier and breathing in his intoxicating scent. Those kinds of thoughts needed to be banished before they landed her in trouble.

"And, for the record," he continued with a devilish grin, "there's nothing funny about the way I handle business."

She grinned. She knew he was joking just to keep things light between them. "I'll keep that in mind. But as far as climbing into your bed, with or without you being there? That won't be necessary. I'm an early riser, too. Besides, I'll need to get to work."

"I thought you took a week off for our honeymoon."

"I did." A honeymoon that would at least in part be spent moving her belongings into Daniel's home. It wasn't exactly romantic, but then, this wasn't a romance. "But I was talking about later. When the honeymoon is over."

He nodded. "That makes sense. I'm usually not this dense. I don't know what's wrong with me right now."

From her perspective, there was nothing wrong with him. But then, she was staring at his bare torso. Or, more specifically, his sculpted shoulders and biceps. When her mouth started to water at the very thought of feeling those strong arms around her in a tight embrace, she knew it was time to grab her nightgown and go.

Once the gown was firmly in her hand, she bade Daniel good-night and dashed through the bathroom to her bedroom. She didn't realize she'd been holding her breath the entire time until it whooshed out of her. She slipped into the scrap of silk and lace her mother had insisted was perfect for her wedding night and then hopped into bed, where she knew she wouldn't sleep a wink. This was going to be one long night.

Chapter Thirteen

Daniel listened to the silence coming from the other bedroom. He'd been awake for an hour, yet he hadn't gotten out of bed, which was unusual for him. Once he awoke, he always climbed out of bed and got to work. There weren't enough hours in the day to get everything done—especially since Hailey had come to live with him—so lying in bed, doing nothing, was a luxury he couldn't afford. Still, today, he didn't move.

Closing his eyes, he pictured how Brittany had looked yesterday at their wedding. She'd been so beautiful. So sexy. Her eyes had sparkled with excitement as they'd danced. And last night, wearing only a navy-blue towel, she'd been a vision. It had taken every ounce of strength he'd possessed to keep from unwrapping the towel from her body and letting it drop to the floor. Of course, doing so would have violated their agreement. He couldn't afford to step across the line. Not just because of Hailey, although her welfare was primary, but because of the kind of man he was.

His word was his bond. He didn't give it easily, but when he made a promise, he kept it. He wouldn't change that now. Dragging a hand down his face, he got out of bed. There was plenty to do and time was a-wasting.

Today he and Brittany were moving her belongings into his house. Although her condo could fit into his house several times over, he had a feeling that adding whatever furniture and other items she wanted to bring to his place wasn't going to be as simple as it sounded. Sure, he had the space, but items with sentimental value deserved places of honor. He wanted Brittany to feel at home in his house. If that meant being surrounded by her knickknacks, so be it.

A knock on his door pulled him away from his musings.

"You decent?" Brittany called from the other side of the door.

That depended on what she meant by decent. If she meant his thoughts—hell no. Just hearing her voice sent them veering into the X-rated. But if she was talking about his appearance? Maybe.

When Hailey had come to live with him, he'd begun sleeping in pajama bottoms. No matter how hard he tried, he couldn't make himself wear the tops. The bottoms were confining enough as it was.

"Sure." She'd seen his chest before and hadn't fainted. In fact, she'd seemed to like what she'd seen. But then again, he could be projecting how he'd felt seeing her nearly nude.

The door opened and Brittany stepped inside. He took one look at her and his heart practically jumped out of his chest. She was dressed in a pink silk-and-lace nightgown that revealed as much as it covered. For a brief moment, he was willing to throw his dignity and self-respect into a burning Dumpster and enjoy a few hours in his bed with her.

Oblivious to the thoughts he was currently battling, Brittany smiled then crossed the room and sat on his bed. Her sweet scent teased his nostrils. "I was in such a rush last night that I forgot to grab clothes for today."

Apparently she was in no rush to get them because she didn't move toward his closet.

Looking at her beautiful face made thinking hard, but looking at her body made thinking impossible. So he focused on her feet. That should be safe. After all, there was absolutely nothing attractive about toes. One glance had him rethinking that belief. Because her feet were sexy as hell. She'd painted her toenails the same pink color as her fingernails. The skin of her feet was smooth brown and looked soft and touchable. He imagined his feet tangled up with hers and realized there was no distracting himself from his desire for her. The only way to keep from acting on his lust was to stay busy.

"Go ahead and get them," he urged. "I'll get dressed, too. We need to pick up Hailey from your parents. I don't want her worrying that I forgot about her." His voice came out harsher than he'd intended. But it was hard to sound friendly when he was fighting to keep his hands to himself.

"Okay." The hurt and shock in her eyes made his stomach twist with guilt. Just because he was struggling with desire didn't give him the right to be rude to her. His lust was his problem.

"I'm sorry. I didn't mean to be sharp."

"Sure. I doubt that Hailey's awake now, but if she is, she's in great hands. I have no doubt that my parents are spoiling her rotten. They've been on my case about settling down and giving them grandchildren for a while. Marrying you has gotten them off my back."

"Glad I could help."

"Me, too." She went into the closet, grabbed the outfit that she'd brought with her and was gone, leaving him alone with his thoughts. Not entirely alone. Remnants of her sweet scent hung in the air and teased his senses. He inhaled deeply, basking in the floral scent for a moment before he forced himself to stop fantasizing about Brittany. She was off-limits.

This overwhelming longing was new to him. In the past, if a woman was prohibited for whatever reason, he didn't give her a second thought. His mind and his body had always been in one accord. He'd never fought with himself as he was doing now, never had difficulty staying on the right side of the line. But he'd never been married before, either.

Married. Brittany was his wife to have and to hold as long as they both shall live. If only that were true. Theirs was a marriage in name only, so he didn't picture himself being able to wrap her in his arms any time soon. No, there wouldn't be any holding between them and certainly not any having.

He dressed quickly then went downstairs. Brittany was in the kitchen, leaning against the marble counter and sipping coffee as if she'd done it every day for years. Smiling, she filled a mug and handed it to him. He took a sip. Strong and black, just the way he liked it. While he enjoyed his coffee, he looked at Brittany over the rim of his mug. Dressed in blue denim shorts and a pink T-shirt, she looked sexier than she should have. Her curly hair bounced around her shoulders and his fingers ached to run through it. He could get used to seeing her every morning.

"Are you sure you're dressed for moving furniture?"

Brittany laughed softly and his longing returned with a vengeance. "I'm not moving furniture now. My roommate isn't getting married until later in the fall, so I'll just leave everything there until she moves."

"What about your bedroom furniture?"

"I thought about that. But then I looked around here. All of your rooms are fully furnished. There's really no space for my stuff. I could put my bed and dresser in storage, but that really doesn't make sense. Amanda can turn my room into a guest room."

He nodded. That was quite generous of her, but not surprising. Brittany was a very generous and giving person. If there was a selfish bone in her body, he hadn't discovered it.

Not that he believed she was perfect. He didn't. Everyone had flaws, himself included. But Brittany had to be as close to perfect as anyone he'd ever met. That, given his growing attraction to her, wasn't a good thing. He needed her to have more faults. Not the kind that would make living with her difficult, but those that would stem his attraction to her before it got the better of him.

"I just need to pick up my clothes and small items. Everything should fit in the back of your SUV. I think it would be better to leave Hailey with my parents instead of trying to do this with her, but it's obviously up to you."

He nodded. "Let's check with your parents then decide. If Hailey is fine, there's no reason to disturb her. But if she's missing me, we can pick her up."

"That makes sense." Brittany finished her coffee, rinsed her mug and then set it in the sink. She looked at the wall clock. "I thought you said your employees arrive at seven."

"I gave them the week off. I figured it would be easier to convince people that we were enjoying our honeymoon if we spent the week alone. Getting used to living together will be hard enough without an audience."

She nodded. "You think of everything. And thank you. I'll feel better knowing I'm not being watched."

He downed his coffee then called her parents and spoke with his mother-in-law. He could hear Hailey chattering and laughing in the background, so he knew that she was happy for the time being. Mallory promised to call him if Hailey started to fuss.

"She okay?" Brittany asked when he ended the call.

"Yes. So I'm ready whenever you are."

"I'm ready now. Just let me grab my purse."

Five minutes later, they were in his SUV on the way to her apartment. He'd been there a couple of times, but since theirs wasn't a real relationship, he'd never entered her bedroom. Now he would be walking into the inner sanctum. Despite telling himself they wouldn't be doing anything other than grabbing the belongings she'd chosen to take with her, his heart sped up at the thought.

It was warm, so they'd rolled down the windows to let in the sweet breeze. Birds chirped in the trees, their music filling the air. Despite the beautiful day, he was acutely aware of Brittany sitting beside him and his heart thumped. He reached out to caress her face. Luckily he realized what he was doing in the nick of time and turned on the radio instead, disguising his original action.

He didn't necessarily feel like listening to music—he generally preferred to drive in silence—but he needed the distraction. Brittany hummed along to the song, then began to sing. Though he had a decent if unremarkable voice, he'd never felt comfortable singing in front of others. Brittany had no such reluctance and she sang quite loudly and with gusto. He had to give her credit for boldness.

If he had as hard a time staying on key as she did, he wouldn't even sing in the shower.

Maybe that was the flaw he'd been searching for? No. Instead of being annoyed, he found her lack of talent endearing.

Once they reached her apartment, he parked in the underground lot and they took the elevator to her floor. She looked around as they walked through the hallway to her front door. She slowed, as if saying goodbye to a home she'd loved. He wouldn't pretend to know what she was feeling, but he could let her know he was there for her. Reaching out, he grabbed her hand and gave it a gentle squeeze.

"I'm okay," she murmured as they stepped inside. "I packed up the kitchen. I don't cook much but, believe it or not, I have a full set of pots and pans and a bunch of gadgets that I never use. I also have my great-aunt's good china. She gave it to me when she moved into a retirement home. I was born on her birthday, so she always favored me. Crazy, huh?"

"You never know what makes people tick."

There was no way he would judge her aunt. He didn't know much about marriage, but he knew criticizing the in-laws never led to anyplace good.

"I guess. She was angry with my mother for a long time because she thought Mom should have named me after her. My mother swore she didn't know it was my great-aunt's birthday."

"What's her name?"

"Grace." Brittany took a step around him and tripped over a box.

He laughed at the irony. "I can see that," he teased. "Was your middle name supposed to have been ballerina?"

She punched him in the arm, which only made him laugh harder. She frowned before she laughed with him.

He added a sense of humor and the ability to laugh at herself to the ever-growing list of qualities he admired about her. At this rate, he'd be able to fill a notebook before the day was over.

They carried down the boxes she'd filled

and then headed back up to her bedroom. "I know I should have packed up my clothes and shoes, but I ran out of time."

"No worries."

He stripped her bed and turned to drop the linens into a box as Brittany grabbed a fistful of lacy underwear from her top drawer. Their eyes met and her cheeks grew pink as she tossed her frilly panties into a box. She opened another drawer and began grabbing socks, avoiding his gaze as she emptied the drawers.

When her dresser was empty, she went to work on the walk-in closet, pulling out armfuls of dresses. Had she really told him that all of her belongings could fit in his SUV? Not with the amount of clothes she had. And she didn't appear to be anywhere near finished with the closet.

Not that he was judging the size of her wardrobe. He'd once been a part of the corporate world and knew the importance of projecting the right image. And if she owned all of these outfits simply because she liked to look good? More power to her.

It took several hours to pack up her belongings and three trips to his ranch, but finally part one of moving her in had been accomplished. Putting things away would be more her job than his. It was up to Brittany to decide what went where.

He didn't have any emotional ties to any of his household furnishings. He'd hired a designer to decorate, so nothing had sentimental value. He'd already told Brittany she had free rein to rearrange the furniture or replace items with her own. More than anything, he wanted her to be happy and comfortable, making his home hers.

Once the boxes were piled inside the house, he put the car seat back into the SUV and they headed to Brittany's parents' house to pick up his daughter. As they neared his in-laws' neighborhood his excitement grew. Although it had only been a day, less than that, really, he'd missed Hailey. It hadn't taken long for her to become the most important part of his life. He loved her more than anything in the world and would do anything for her. His marriage was proof of that.

He parked and turned off the ignition. Brittany was reaching for her door handle when he stopped her.

"What?" she asked, looking genuinely perplexed. Then she shot him a mischievous look. "Don't tell me you want to carry me over my parents' threshold, too?"

He laughed. "No. There's no tradition for that."

"Good. That would have been a bit excessive."

"Your parents believe we're newlyweds."

"Technically, we are. At least, that's what you keep telling me." The smirk on her face was cute and he grinned.

"My point is that we need to look and behave like newlyweds."

"You lost me. I know how to act like a new bride, but I have no idea how a new bride looks."

He paused. They had a deal, but still…this was important.

"They hold hands and are affectionate. I need you to feel comfortable with me touching you in front of your parents. I might hug you or kiss you and I don't want you to pull away."

Her cheeks pinked up, but she nodded. "I can do that."

"I know."

He held out his hand and she took it for a moment. Her skin was warm and soft, and he hated to let it go. But he had to…to get out of the car. Once they were out, he wrapped his arm around her waist and pulled her closer to him. He liked the feel of her by his side.

The front door opened before they were up the steps. Mallory stood there, holding Hailey. When his daughter saw him, she let out a happy squeal and lunged for him. He trotted up the last step and scooped Hailey into his arms. He hugged her and she giggled then gave him a sloppy kiss on his cheek. Daniel reached out and took Brittany's hand, pulling her into a family hug. For something that was a sham, he couldn't help but think that it felt so right.

Brittany watched the reunion between father and daughter with a happy heart. The love between Hailey and Daniel was so real. So strong. It would be cruel for the courts to separate them.

"Come on in," her mother said. "Do you have time to visit?"

Brittany met Daniel's gaze. Though he didn't say anything, she could read in his eyes that he would do what she wanted, but she knew that he really wanted to just go home. "Not today. I want to get settled. And I'm sure Hailey would like to be in her own home and play with her toys."

"Okay. But Hailey had a good time with her nana and grandpops."

At the sound of her name, Hailey turned and looked at Mallory. She babbled a few words then lay her head against Daniel's chest. Clearly, Hailey was ready for the fun time she'd had with her new grandparents to come to an end.

Once they were back in the SUV, Hailey began babbling and she chattered all the way to the ranch.

"I thought babies were supposed to fall asleep in the car," Brittany said.

Daniel laughed. "Not after a nap, which I suspect Hailey has just had."

Great. Apparently, Brittany's full-time mommy duty was going to start immediately with a wide-awake baby.

When they got to the ranch—home, she reminded herself—Daniel took Hailey out of her car seat and grabbed the diaper bag in one smooth motion. Daniel might not have had a baby for long, but he'd mastered some essential skills.

When Hailey spotted the maze of boxes, she was instantly intrigued and struggled to get out of Daniel's arms. Sighing, he put her down and they watched as she crawled to the nearest one and used it to help her stand.

Daniel smiled over at Brittany and her heart

lurched. What was that about? She knew she was attracted to him, but if a simple smile could make her heart soar to the sky, she was in danger. Danger of falling in love with him. And under no circumstance could she fall in love with him. What she and Daniel had was a business arrangement and it would behoove her to remember that. When the time came for their marriage to end, she would pack up and leave, returning to her regularly scheduled life while he went back to his. She couldn't afford to let herself have romantic feelings for him. To do so would be disastrous.

A part of her still couldn't believe she'd actually married him. Sure, the idea of having the funds to start her own business had been tempting. As the child of business owners, she'd always wanted to work for herself and be the one in control, the one making the rules and the important decisions. But marrying to achieve that goal was completely out of character for her.

Could it be that there had been something

at work in her subconscious? Did she secretly want to be married and have a baby? Not married to Daniel, of course, but married to an imaginary perfect husband.

This marriage was a convenient way to try her hand at being someone's wife and mother; a way to discover if she was cut out for the job. One might say she was trying on the role to see how it fit. If she liked how it felt, she might adjust her five-year plan for her life, penciling in marriage. And if she didn't like it, she could cross that off her to-do list and carry on as planned. She didn't kid herself that it would be as easy as returning an unworn dress, but it was the best she could do. She didn't actually believe she would decide she wanted a husband and kids, but this way she'd be sure she wasn't missing out.

As she watched Hailey tumble onto her diapered bottom, Brittany felt a flood of emotions. She really cared about Hailey and wanted her to have a great future. A happy life. The best way to accomplish that was to live with Daniel.

Hailey enjoyed playing for a few more minutes then, without warning, her pleasure vanished, and she dropped to the floor and began to fuss.

He picked up Hailey and held her against his chest. "I was about to carry the boxes upstairs, but I guess that can wait."

Brittany looked at her new daughter. She was going to have to step into the role as mother sooner or later. Start as You Intend to Continue applied here, too. "Let me take her. She might need a diaper change. Or want a snack."

"Are you sure?"

"Yes. You just get those boxes where they belong, Muscle Man."

"Muscle Man?" He smiled and preened, flexing his biceps.

Why had she said that out loud? The man didn't need to be reminded of what he looked like. There were mirrors in this house. Not to mention women in this town who weren't nearly as discreet as Brittany wished they were. She'd seen women turn and stare when

Daniel came into view. There was no way he'd missed it, either.

"Don't let it go to your head. Your muscles are bigger than mine and therefore better suited to physical labor like carrying."

"I see." He winked at her and then bent to pick up a box, putting it on his shoulder. Though she tried not to look, her eyes drifted down to his backside, which, she noticed, was also toned. She forced her eyes upward across his back and shoulders. She didn't know what kind of regimen this man had, but it was working. She'd need to up her game if she wanted to look as good as he did.

But why? This wasn't a competition. And he wasn't going to be seeing her naked anyway.

Hailey began to make louder noises, stirring Brittany out of her silly musings. "Let's get you a new diaper."

Brittany and Daniel walked to the stairs. He paused and swept out his free arm. "After you."

Suddenly self-conscious, Brittany climbed

the stairs with a bit of a sidestep. Then she decided to heck with that and put a little extra swing into her hips. He wolf-whistled and she wondered if she was playing with fire. Maybe, but she was going to be living here for a while. She and Daniel needed to be able to have fun together. After all, there was that social worker to fool. As well as the judge. And the more comfortable they were together, the better their charade would be.

At least, that was what she told herself. Because anything else was unthinkable.

Chapter Fourteen

Brittany dropped onto the sofa beside Daniel and tucked her feet beneath her. She couldn't remember the last time she'd been this exhausted. Hailey had positively worn her out. There'd been moments when she'd wanted to wave the white flag and cry uncle, letting the little girl know she'd won. But she'd been determined to prove to Daniel that he could trust her with Hailey.

Taking care of a baby was a lot harder than her cousins had made it look. But then, none of them had started out with a nine-month-old. They'd learned how to care for babies with infants who didn't crawl away the second you turned your back. None of their first days had been with teething kids who fussed and drooled and gummed everything in sight. Most of Brittany's exhaustion was a result of being on alert for hours on end. If she wasn't checking to make sure that Hailey wasn't about to pull something onto her head or crawl down the stairs, she was watching to be sure that the baby didn't shove something into her mouth. Or nose. Or ears.

But Hailey was now fed, bathed, freshly diapered and sound asleep in her crib where, hopefully, she would sleep through the night. Though it was only eight o'clock, Brittany longed to fall into bed herself. But that would look like she hadn't been up to the task. Daniel, on the other hand, looked fresh as a daisy and not like he'd been carrying boxes around all evening. No, she needed to stay awake for at least two more hours. Ten o'clock or bust.

"Thanks for putting my stuff away," she said then yawned.

"No worries. I needed some special china

for the cabinet. The designer had offered to purchase some for me, but I hadn't been interested then. Now I like the way the dishes look in there. I'll have to get some when you move out."

She nodded. Aunt Grace's dishes did look like they'd been made especially for the cabinet. But Brittany couldn't concentrate on china, not after what Daniel had said. *When you move out.* She didn't want to think about her marriage ending. Not tonight.

"So what do you want to do now?"

He looked surprised by her question. "You aren't tired? I love Hailey to pieces, but taking care of her full-time wears me out. But then, you helped your mother with your brothers and sisters, so you have more experience than I do."

She allowed herself to sink deeper into the sofa cushions and released the sigh she'd been stifling. If they were going to have a successful marriage, she needed to answer his questions honestly. That is, as long as the questions didn't involve her growing attraction to him. "Truthfully, she wore me out, too. And I don't ever remember being this exhausted."

"How about we warm up the takeout and eat here while we watch TV?" They'd stopped at DJ's Deluxe on the way home from picking up Hailey and had grabbed a ton of food.

"That sounds good to me."

"You stay here. I'll get it."

He wouldn't get any argument from her. Just the idea of being waited on hand and foot was enough to make her heart smile.

Daniel was back in a few minutes, carrying two overflowing plates. The aroma alone made her mouth water. Daniel set the plates on the coffee table and went back to the kitchen. He returned momentarily, carrying a bottle of wine and two glasses in his hands, two water bottles tucked under his arms.

A minute later they were holding plates on their laps and trying to find something they would both enjoy watching on television. When they couldn't agree on anything, he switched off the TV and turned on the stereo. Fortunately they were both fans of seventies music.

They talked easily while they ate. Brittany was surprised to discover how well they got along. She couldn't remember the last time she'd had so much fun with a man. They'd told funny stories from their childhood and teen years, and Brittany had been endlessly amused by tales of his antics. He reminded her so much of her brothers that she felt as if she'd known him all her life. There was definitely more to Daniel than he let on. Under other circumstances, she'd want to get to closer to him to see where things led. But being temporarily married made that permanently impossible. Still, there was no reason they couldn't enjoy their time together for however long it lasted.

She sipped her wine then looked over at him. "Why Montana? I can understand leaving a successful business you'd started in order to try something new, but why move to an entirely different state?"

He leaned back against the sofa and paused

as if weighing his next words before uttering them. "Moving to Montana was about more than business. I was at a place in my life where I needed a total change. There's so much untapped potential here. The possibilities for growth are endless. But that's just business.

"On a personal note, I needed the space to breathe. And the natural beauty here is unrivaled. I also liked the idea of setting down roots in Bronco. Now that I have Hailey, I know I've made the right decision."

"I grew up in this town and I love it, so you'll get no argument from me about the natural beauty. We're surrounded by it."

His eyes swept over her and she felt her cheeks warm. "I certainly am."

Just like that, the mood turned sensual. A part of Brittany wanted to flirt back. And more. What harm would there be in a few kisses? After all, they were married. And they knew where to draw the line. She knew Daniel's character. He was a gentleman and would take no for an answer. That wasn't the issue. The problem was that, right now, in the dimly lit room with the soft music playing in the background, and feeling relaxed from the wine, Brittany wasn't confident she would say no.

She decided that a wise woman wouldn't put her self-control to the test, so she polished off her wine, set her glass on the table and met Daniel's gaze. The warmth she saw there had her coming close to reconsidering her stand. "Thanks for a lovely evening. I have a feeling that Hailey will be up bright and early tomorrow, meaning we should be, too. So I guess I'll say good-night now."

Standing, she reached for the dishes. He rose, too, and put his hand on hers. Silly tingles skittered down her spine. She tried to convince herself they were the result of the wine and not from the feel of his skin on hers, but she knew that wasn't true. Their gazes met and her breath caught in her throat. For a moment, she thought he might kiss her and her heart sped up with delicious anticipation. Instead, he gave his head a little shake and then dropped his hand. She forced a smile, masking her disappointment.

"I'll take care of the dishes."

Right. The dishes. Odd how she'd forgotten what she'd intended to do just that easily. It was definitely time to end the night. "Thanks. I'll see you in the morning."

She walked from the room on wobbly knees, feeling his eyes on her. She climbed the stairs sedately even though she wanted to race up them like there was a prize waiting for the winner.

Once she reached her room, she sat on her bed and the air whooshed from her lungs. She needed to get a handle on her attraction. How many times did she need to tell herself that Daniel was off-limits before her body got the message?

Daniel looked out the window and frowned. Rain was coming down in buckets. His plan for the three of them to go into town and spend the day together had been washed away by the weather. It looked like he and Brittany would be alone again today. Of course, Hailey would be with them, but she wasn't much of a chaperone. And given his growing attraction to Brittany, it would be nice to have someone else around whose presence would force him to behave.

He knew that flirting with Brittany wasn't wise or in either of their best interests. He hadn't thought that refraining would be a problem. He'd never been much of a flirt in the first place, preferring the direct approach. That way, there were no misunderstandings. If a woman was interested, great. If not, she could say so and he would move on. No harm, no foul. But for some reason he had yet to discover, he caught himself flirting and dropping hints with Brittany. His behavior was out of character and it confused the heck out of him.

Beautiful as she was, he wasn't interested in dating her. They didn't want the same things. She was focused on building a business, not a family. She didn't want kids. He had a nine-month-old. And though Brittany was willing to help him in the short term, she'd made it plain that she didn't want anything permanent. Given that he'd done his share of rejecting women in the past, he wasn't upset with her.

Yet knowing that she didn't see him playing a role in her future hadn't diminished his attraction to her. It was just as strong as ever. And growing. That's why he'd planned to go into town. She was just so appealing that being alone with her would only lead to trouble.

He swiped a hand over his forehead as he recalled being alone with her last night. The urge to kiss her had nearly overwhelmed him…until he remembered their deal. This was a business-arrangement marriage and not a love match. Kissing and any other shows of affection would only muddy the waters. It was in their best interests that they stick to the rules they'd established.

This entire marriage was more complicated than he'd expected it to be. But since they'd already said their vows in front of scores of witnesses, there was no turning around now. And, truthfully, he didn't want to do things differently. Because, right or wrong, wise or foolish, he was attracted to his bride. Though it had only been a couple of days, he enjoyed being married to her.

"Do you think the rain will stop soon?" Brittany asked, coming into the room, Hailey in her arms. Dressed in what she referred to as cowgirl chic—pink denim shorts, a pink, green and white plaid shirt, and pink-and-white sandals—she made his heart flutter.

She came to stand beside him and look out the window. Her familiar scent wafted under his nose and his imagination switched into overdrive. Her perfume had a vaguely floral scent that appealed to him. But it was her personal scent that turned him on and had him fantasizing about ways for them to entertain themselves here.

"Ba baboo," Hailey said, reaching for him.

"Did you two have fun?"

"That's one word for it," Brittany said dryly.

"I told you I would take care of her today."

"I know, and I had fully intended to take you up on that offer. But one thing turned into another and time got away from us. Besides, we were having fun playing with her stuffed animals. And I know you had work to do."

Truer words were never spoken. When he'd worked at his company, he'd been able to delegate a lot of tasks to his staff. He'd also had complete departments dedicated to advertising and promotion as well as business development. That was no longer the case. He was now an army of one. True, he'd hired Brittany to handle the affair on behalf of his resort, but he was still responsible for every other aspect of its launch. He had the money to hire a full complement of employees, but he didn't want to do that. He relished doing most things on his own and stretching different creative muscles.

"Thanks. I got more done today than I had in a long time, which is why I was planning an outing for this afternoon. The rain has put a damper on that."

"So let's do something else. We might not be able to go outside, but we can have a good time inside."

"Doing what?"

She looked so cute with her furrowed brow as she thought. "I don't know. Hailey just woke up from her nap, so she needs to eat. And I'm a bit hungry myself."

His stomach growled then, saving him from uttering his agreement. But since he'd given his staff the week off, he and Brittany were in charge of cooking, something neither of them did particularly well. "What would you like?"

"What do you have?"

He knew he had a good supply of baby food, but other than that? He didn't have the foggiest idea. Hopefully, his cook had left something in the freezer that they could just warm up. Otherwise they were on their own, something he didn't relish.

While he strapped Hailey into her high chair, Brittany rummaged in the pantry, coming out with a jar of baby food and a biscuit that his daughter loved. While Brittany heated the baby food, he scrounged through the freezer, but nothing he found appealed to him.

"There's nothing to eat," he said.

"Oh. So what's the plan?"

"I guess I could go out for something."

"How about ordering a pizza? Or wings?"

"You'd be okay with that?"

"Of course."

He didn't know why he was surprised by her response. Brittany had showed him on more than one occasion that although she dressed nicely and seemed to enjoy the finer things in life, she wasn't pretentious or demanding.

"I'll call in an order and then swing by to pick it up."

"Okay. Sounds good."

"Or, if you want, you and Hailey can come with me."

"Sort of a family outing, after all?"

It wasn't what he'd had in mind, but it still had appeal. "Yes."

"I'm in. Let me finish feeding Hailey and then we'll be ready to go."

He nodded and watched as Brittany tried to convince Hailey to eat her food.

When Hailey'd first started eating, she'd opened her mouth in anticipation. That was no longer the case. Now she turned her head away whenever Brittany offered her the spoon. She wanted to feed herself. Only, the spoon held little interest for her. She preferred to use her fingers.

Though he knew first-hand how exasperating it could be when Hailey chose not to cooperate, he found the entire scene amusing. But as determined as Hailey was to do things her way, Brittany was just as determined.

"I don't know why she's acting like this. She didn't do this before."

"She's practicing being a woman," he said with a chuckle.

Brittany's hand froze, spoon in the air. "Say what?"

Uh-oh. "She's just not feeling it, so she's exercising her feminine prerogative of expressing her feelings honestly." When Brittany only stared at him, he swallowed. He knew he should stop talking, lest he dig himself a deeper hole, but he continued, hoping for a way out. "She's being her authentic self, which is something we should honor."

"I see." Brittany turned back to the baby, but he could see there was a smile on her face. He didn't know whether it was because she was pleased by what he'd said or because Hailey had decided that she wanted to use the spoon. Whatever the reason, Brittany's joy touched his heart in a way that could be described with one word. Dangerous. Her happiness shouldn't matter that much to him. And it certainly shouldn't make him feel all warm and gooey inside.

"It looks like we're done here," Brittany said, interrupting his musings. "Give me ten minutes and we'll be ready to go."

He nodded. The idea of being in the close confines of the SUV with Brittany was simultaneously thrilling and nerve-racking. He tried to find a neutral emotion but couldn't think of one, so he would just have to be thrilled, which was, in and of itself, nerve-racking.

He really was losing it. But what a way to go.

Chapter Fifteen

Daniel was focused on driving, so Brittany took the opportunity to study him without getting caught. He looked so calm and cool, steering the SUV through the streets. He was dressed in a gray shirt that hugged his torso and jeans that fit his muscular thighs. His appearance set her imagination free and she hoped her reaction didn't show on her face. Though she'd been around him many times over the past weeks, she hadn't found a way to inoculate herself to his appeal. Despite all her rational arguments why becoming emotionally or physically involved with him was a bad idea, her stubborn body zinged whenever he was near. And in the intimate confines of the vehicle, her body was lighting up like the classic pinball machine languishing in her parents' basement.

She had hoped that having Hailey around would temper her body's response, but the little girl's presence didn't make an impact. Brittany's insides were humming a happy tune. Worse, her hands ached to run up and down his muscular arms. Not sure how long she could resist the urge, she folded her hands together as if in prayer.

The rain had slowed and it was barely drizzling when they reached the pizza parlor. Daniel held an umbrella over Hailey and Brittany as they entered the restaurant. The place was filled with people who'd had the same idea, but there were a couple of free tables. They had no problem switching from carryout to dining in. A waitress brought them their hot pizza at the same time she brought their cold drinks.

Brittany settled Hailey into a high chair and

gave her a couple of toys that she'd no doubt pick up several times before the night was over.

Daniel was as charming as ever and even a bit flirtatious. Brittany found herself flirting in return, something she'd told herself not to do but couldn't seem to stop. Their hands touched often, as was the case when two people shared a pizza, and she was aware of every touch. Every glance. She noticed every little thing about him. The way his eyes squinted when he laughed. The dimple in his right cheek.

"Well, if it's not the newlyweds," a female voice called.

Brittany turned and smiled at her friend. Rising, she gave Melanie Driscoll a hug. "What a surprise seeing you here."

"I was in the mood for pizza, so Gabe and I decided to brave the rain." She grinned and winked. "Don't tell DJ."

Brittany laughed. Her friend was the new CFO of DJ's Incorporated. "Your secret is safe with me."

"Do you want to join us?" Daniel asked, offering his seat to Melanie.

"No, we're getting ours to go." She looked over her shoulder at her fiancé, Gabe Abernathy, who was holding a pizza box over by the door. "I just wanted to say hello. I miss seeing you now that we're no longer neighbors."

"We'll have to have lunch soon."

"I'm going to hold you to that."

"Give our best to Gabe."

"I will." Melanie took a step then turned back around. "You three really are a beautiful family."

"That couldn't have worked out better if I had planned it," Daniel said after Melanie had walked away.

"Planned what?"

"Running into your friends. Being seen together as a family. We can't stay secluded on the ranch, no matter how much I would like to. We need to be out and about together. It's important that people believe we're a real family and that we belong together."

"Of course," Brittany agreed then took a

bite of her pizza. What had been a perfect combination of spicy tomato sauce, gooey cheese and savory sausage now tasted like ashes. She'd been enjoying the evening with Daniel, even the flirting. Especially the flirting. And all the while he'd thinking about how being seen as a besotted husband would work to his advantage.

Brittany forced herself to snap out of it. They had an agreement with terms specifically spelled out. Just because she wasn't as certain as she'd been a couple of weeks ago didn't give her to right to renegotiate the contract to something that suited her current desires. As a businesswoman she knew a deal was a deal.

So she swallowed her bitterness along with the pizza and adjusted her attitude. If Daniel wanted to convince the town they were in love, that's what she would do.

When they'd finished eating, they boxed up the leftovers and stood. Hailey reached for Brittany and she automatically picked her up. Daniel grabbed the doggie bag with one hand and put the other one on Brittany's waist. His hand was warm and the heat permeated her skin and all but melted her bones. She leaned against her husband just as any new bride would, then concentrated on not going up in smoke.

The ride home was uneventful and Brittany used the time to remind herself that she and Daniel had a plan that included the dinner he'd hired her to arrange. She'd spent so much time organizing the wedding that Daniel's event had fallen by the wayside. It was time to remove it from the back burner and give it the attention it deserved.

When they got home, they played with Hailey for a while. Daniel tossed the baby into the air several times and she laughed loudly. Clearly, she was having the time of her life.

Though Brittany had never dated men with children for obvious reasons, she loved watching Daniel interact with the baby. He was so gentle, giving her one hundred percent of his attention. Her happiness and well-being were the most important things in the world to him. Suddenly the sexiest thing about Daniel wasn't his washboard abs or massive chest. It was the way he adored Hailey.

That thought puzzled her. If she didn't want children, and in fact wasn't sure she even wanted a husband, why did the fact that Daniel would make a great father appeal to her so much? Why did her stomach do loop-de-loops when she heard him sing silly songs or watched him play peek-a-boo with Hailey?

Her changing priorities worried her. She was more at ease when her attraction was limited to his physical attributes. She was even okay with admiring his ambition and business acumen. That was safe. But being pulled to him because of the way he enjoyed being a father? Her heart was skating on thin ice with that one. Too bad it wasn't something she could control.

She'd been lost in thought awhile and it took her a minute to realize the laughter had stopped. Turning, she looked at the floor where Daniel and Hailey had been playing. Now they were sprawled across the blanket.

Daniel was lying on his back, his eyes closed. Hailey was lying across his chest, her thumb in her mouth. Brittany's heart squeezed at the sight.

Daniel's eyes opened and he caught her staring at him. She just hoped he couldn't see her emotions in her eyes.

"Let me help you," she said, lifting Hailey from his chest then holding the baby against her own.

"Thanks."

He stood in one graceful moment. "I guess she wore herself out."

"It looked to me like both of you were asleep."

"Nah. I have energy to spare. It takes more than playing with a little girl to wear me out."

Brittany pressed her lips together to keep any inappropriate words from escaping. Instead she rocked back and forth, hoping the motion would keep Hailey asleep until she was in her crib. When Brittany was certain she wasn't going to suggest they burn off their excess energy together in the way most newlyweds did, she spoke. "I'll be right back. I'm going to put her to bed."

Daniel's smile was both mischievous and mysterious and her self-control wavered. Only a moment. Then she forced herself to remember the dinner that was supposed to launch his business as well as catapult her career.

"When I come back, I want to discuss your event. We need to kick the planning into high gear."

Was that disappointment on his face? It couldn't be. Their relationship had started because of the dinner and his dude ranch. She might be his temporary wife, but she was still his event planner.

After she'd settled Hailey, Brittany went back downstairs. Daniel hadn't picked up the blanket, but instead was sitting on it. He looked extremely relaxed reclining against the sofa, his legs stretched out in front of him. He looked even more tantalizing than the tray of fruit and cheese beside the bottle of wine on the table.

He gave her a lazy grin. "I know it's a meeting, but nothing says we have to do it at a desk."

"I don't recall any of our other meetings being this casual."

"Really? Don't tell me you've forgotten about our horse ride already. I'm devastated."

She laughed and sat beside him. Before coming downstairs, she'd stopped in her room to grab the file. Regardless of the setting and the sexual attraction arcing between them, she intended to conduct herself professionally.

Reaching into her notebook, she flipped to a page of suggestions she'd jotted down. She began to explain them to Daniel along with the reasons she'd chosen the path she had. After ten minutes where she was the only one doing the talking, she looked at him. He'd never been so reticent in the past. "Don't you have anything to say?"

"Everything sounds good."

"That's it? You don't want to change anything? You weren't this easygoing before."

He shrugged. "My situation is different now than it was when I first hired you."

She hoped that didn't mean he'd lost interest in the project. She was planning to use it to showcase her skills and convince Cornelius Taylor to hire her. This dinner was a steppingstone to greater things. "How?"

"I'm married now."

"I know. I was there."

"I'm new to being a husband, so I don't know everything." He paused as he rubbed his chin.

She wished he would just get to it. "We have the same amount of time in the marriage game."

"Well, there is a well-known saying. Happy wife, happy life. So if you like it, I love it."

"That's it?" She was flabbergasted. He'd given her such a hard time before. Now that they were married, he no longer had an opinion? She couldn't name the emotions that coursed through her body, but she was fairly certain that none of them were positive. She didn't want favoritism. She wanted her work taken seriously. She wanted to be respected as the professional that she was.

"As flattering as that may be," she said, not bothering to mask the displeasure in her voice, "I'd rather you look at what I've done in the same way you would if we weren't married. I put a lot of effort into this project and I want you to give it proper consideration."

"But we are married and I can't pretend that we aren't."

"But it's not a real marriage."

"It's real enough."

"Regardless, I want your input. You made it clear that this dinner is very important to you and your business. I want it to be everything you envision it to be."

"Okay. But you told me that you could deliver what no one else could. That you are the best at what you do. I already had faith in you and your talent. I wouldn't have hired you otherwise. You wanted me to trust you and now that I do, you aren't happy."

"I still want you to trust my abilities. But I

want you to be honest about my plans. I want you to be satisfied with the dinner. If there's something that you don't like, say so. My feelings won't be hurt. I don't want you agreeing just to make your little woman happy. I need you to separate the business from the personal. Can you do that?"

"Certainly, Mrs. Dubois."

She rolled her eyes. "Who said I was going to change my name?"

"No one. It's your right to use whichever name you want."

She nodded. She really hadn't given her name serious thought. And she wasn't going to think about it now. Right now she was going to focus on work.

Once they'd cleared the air, it was easy to get down to business. They discussed her plan in detail and Daniel suggested a few changes. If she thought his idea was better, she altered the plan. If she didn't, she pushed back, which led to quite a few spirited discussions. But when she'd scribbled the last note and closed her file, she was satisfied that they'd come up with the perfect plan. "This is going to be one spectacular dinner."

Daniel smiled. "Yes. Thanks to you. How long will it take to pull it all together?"

"Not long. I've been in contact with several vendors. I just needed your final approval. Now that I have it, I can give everyone the go-ahead."

She started to stand, but he put his hand on hers. "Thank you, Brittany. You've gone above and beyond everything I could have expected. If you weren't my wife and I wasn't afraid of being accused of favoritism, I'd give you a bonus."

"Ah, this marriage is costing me," she joked and then laughed.

He laughed with her, stood and then helped her to her feet. His fingers gripped hers a little longer than necessary before he slowly released her and stepped back. Though disappointed with his withdrawal, she knew it was necessary. They'd established boundaries for a reason. Just because she was attracted to him didn't mean she should start behaving recklessly. In fact, given everything that was at stake, she should reinforce the barriers around her heart before she did something stupid. Like throw herself into his arms and beg him to kiss her the way she'd dreamed of. Dreams were good while you slept but could lead to disaster if acted upon in real life.

"Ah, you've caught on to my devious plan."

"I never took you for a villain."

"Of course, you wouldn't. You're not the suspicious type. If you'd been expecting it, you would have foiled my dastardly plot." He wiggled his eyebrows and twirled a pretend mustache. Then he reached for her and she squealed, barely escaping his grasp.

She grabbed two accent pillows from the sofa, throwing one at him and using the other as a shield.

He dodged the pillow and flashing a devilish grin, he held her gaze as he crossed the room. Her heart pounded as he walked with exaggerated slowness. Out of nowhere, he jumped and grabbed her, pulling her to the couch beside him.

"Now I've got you," he said. He ran his hands down her back, leaving goose bumps in their wake. When they reached her waist, he pulled her close.

She laughed, struggling to keep from wrapping her arms around his neck. Though she was practically overheating, she forced herself to play it cool. "Well, since you caught me, I'll have to wait for my hero to come rescue me."

"He'll never get past my minions."

She longed to stay in his arms—but knew giving in to that desire would only lead to trouble. So she gently pushed him back, letting her hand linger on his shoulder. "Well, while you're holding down the fort, I'm going to soak in a bubble bath. See you in the morning, my villain."

"Not so fast there, my captive bride. You need to convince me to let you walk away." He cupped her jaw and lowered his head to kiss her, and she knew that nothing would stop her from giving in. As she lifted her face to his, the phone rang.

Except that.

"Hold that thought." He looked at the phone's display and his smile vanished. "It's my lawyer."

Daniel spoke for a few tense moments. When the call ended, he looked at her. "The social worker will be coming to see us tomorrow."

Chapter Sixteen

"How do I look?" Brittany asked Daniel as she burst into his office.

He looked up from his desk where he'd been trying, unsuccessfully, to work. This was the third outfit she'd tried on. Each was as beautiful as the one before. The lilac silk blouse and deep purple cropped pants were elegant yet understated. She looked sexy as hell but, given her curves, that wasn't unexpected. Some things couldn't be disguised. "You look great."

She frowned down at herself. "I want to look motherly, but I'm not sure this works.

Maybe I should put the dress back on. Nothing says 'mother' like a peach floral dress."

He grabbed her hand before she could race back upstairs. "You look fine. Not that the social worker will be paying attention to your clothes. What will convince her that we're the right people to raise Hailey is the way we interact with each other. That and how we treat Hailey. We have to make sure this woman knows that we're giving Hailey a happy home so there's no reason to place her with her grandparents."

"This meeting is so important to you. I don't want to blow it."

"You won't. Just be your wonderful self. Act naturally and she won't help but be charmed."

She smiled softly at him and his heart thudded. Though they were putting on this dog and pony show for the social worker, Daniel discovered that he meant every word. Brittany was wonderful and, the social worker would see that, too.

"Thanks."

"Now, how do I look?" he joked.

She laughed, as he'd hoped she would. She was much too tense. Not that he was relaxed by any stretch of the imagination.

Though he ordinarily wore jeans while working on the ranch and a suit in business meetings, he'd put on pressed khakis and a navy button-down shirt. When her eyes traveled over his body, all humor fled him, leaving lust in its wake.

"You'll do," she said, her voice husky. Her cheeks had grown pink and he knew his attraction wasn't one-sided. He put a finger under her chin and tipped her face towards his as he bent down to kiss her. Before their lips could meet, the doorbell rang, and she shot him a panicked look.

The words that might have encouraged her escaped him, so he slipped an arm around her waist, simultaneously giving and receiving comfort.

Brittany grabbed his hand as they walked down the hall. "We can do this."

He smiled. "You bet we can."

They walked to the front door together and

ushered the social worker, who'd introduced herself as Mrs. Kasey, into the front room. He'd imagined the social worker would be a humorless older woman who dressed in bland clothes, sensible shoes and wore her hair pulled in a tight bun in the back of her hair so the woman in her thirties was a surprise.

Despite how friendly the woman seemed, Daniel was suddenly afraid that she'd already decided against them and was merely going through the motions. His little girl was going to be taken away from him by this woman and there was nothing he could do about it.

As if she'd sensed his mind had traveled down a dark road, Brittany squeezed his hand. He glanced at her sweet face and his pounding heart slowed until it beat normally. He squared his shoulders and a sense of purpose and confidence filled him. He wasn't going to give up Hailey without a fight. When the social worker left, she was going to be convinced that he was a loving father who was giving Hailey a good home.

"Welcome to our home," he said.

"Thank you." She looked around the room. Her eyes landed on a framed family photo they'd taken in lieu of engagement photos. "Thank you, Daniel. It's nice to meet you."

"You, too." He introduced Brittany then offered her some refreshment, which she declined. "Would you like to have a seat?"

Mrs. Kasey nodded and sat in the chair he'd indicated. He and Brittany sat side by side on the sofa, still holding hands.

Once they were all settled, Daniel took the lead. "I imagine you want to get right to it. Brittany and I will be happy to answer any questions you have. Hailey is napping now, but she should be awake in half an hour or so."

Mrs. Kasey nodded. "You have a lovely home."

"Thank you," Brittany said. "We're very happy here. I'd be glad to show you around, if you'd like to see more of it."

"That would be nice." Mrs. Kasey pulled a file from her satchel. "I know that the two of you have only recently gotten married. How did that come about?"

Daniel glanced at Brittany, who gave him a warm smile. The look in her eyes was so loving that, for a moment, he could actually believe she was in love with him and not simply pretending. "I'm planning on opening a dude ranch and resort on part of property. I needed to hire an event planner to help with the announcement, so I hired Brittany."

"Actually, he hired a couple of other companies before me," Brittany said, bumping his shoulder with her own and giving him a teasing look before turning back to Mrs. Kasey. "They weren't from here and didn't know the people. Most importantly, they couldn't come up with a plan that Daniel liked."

"True," Daniel said, playing along.

"When he finally decided to hire a local company, I jumped at the chance. I was determined to show him just what I could do. Daniel started out as a challenging client, but it didn't take long for me to discover that he's really a pussycat on the inside."

"Don't let that get out or my reputation as a hardnosed businessman will be ruined."

Brittany laughed and Mrs. Kasey chuckled.

"Anyway," Brittany continued, "we began to spend time together working on his project. As we got to know one another, I fell in love with him."

"And I fell in love with her," Daniel added.

"I see," Mrs. Kasey said, and Daniel wondered just what it was she saw. "You got married rather quickly. Why is that?"

He and Brittany exchanged looks. They'd expected this question and had decided to face it head-on, keeping their answers as close to the truth as possible. That way there was less chance of screwing up and being caught. Now the words he'd rehearsed escaped him. He was still trying to recall his speech when Brittany spoke.

"A couple of reasons. First, neither of us is a kid. I'm thirty-three and Daniel is thirty-six. We've had enough experiences with relationships to know what we want and what we don't. And we know the real thing from imitation. Since we both knew our love was real, there was no reason to wait."

Daniel nodded.

"You said two reasons," Mrs. Kasey said.

"Yes. Hailey was the second and, honestly, the most important. Tragically, she's already lost her parents. She's been through so many changes in her young life, we don't want her to have to endure many more. It's important to us that she have a stable home. Since we knew we loved each other, it seemed better to get married sooner rather than later. That way, I could move in right away and become a regular part of Hailey's life. We want her to know she can count on both of us being here every day."

"And how has she adjusted?"

"She's happy," Daniel said. "She loves Brittany just as much as I do."

Before the social worker could ask another question, Hailey's voice came over the baby monitor.

Brittany and Daniel stood.

"I'll get her," Brittany said and then turned to Mrs. Kasey. "That way you can meet her."

"I'd like that."

Brittany left and Daniel sat back down.

"She's lovely," Mrs. Kasey said.

Daniel's response was honest and heartfelt. "Yes, she is. Before I met Brittany, I didn't believe that a woman as good as she is even existed. You may think it suspicious that we married so soon, but after I got to know her, I was determined not to let her get away. She and Hailey are the best things that have ever happened to me."

"You love her," Mrs. Kasey said as if surprised.

"With all my heart."

Mrs. Kasey nodded and didn't reply. They sat in silence and Daniel got the impression that the social worker was sizing him up. He began to second-guess his answers. Had he blown it by overselling his emotions, claiming to love Brittany with his whole heart? He hoped not. The odd thing was…he hadn't thought before he'd spoken. The words had just come tumbling out of his mouth. Just what did that mean?

Before he could ponder that question and come up with a suitable answer, Brittany was back, Hailey in her arms. She'd dressed Hailey in a cute pink dress with white flowers and matching ruffled bottoms. Brittany had insisted on going shopping for Hailey and they'd come home with bags full of adorable outfits with matching hats and barrettes.

She'd also arranged a photo shoot for the three of them with a photographer she knew. Daniel had been resistant at first, but now he was glad he'd given in. The family pictures scattered around the house added a personal feel to the professionally decorated spaces, something Brittany had known the social worker would look for. The enormous portrait hanging over the living room fireplace was a showstopper. With the other changes Brittany had made, the house truly felt like a home.

Hailey was happily carrying on a one-sided conversation. When she saw him, her eyes lit up and, exclaiming, she reached out to him. His heart melted and he stood, wrapping his arm around Brittany's waist for a second before taking Hailey and holding her against his chest.

He and Brittany sat back down. Hailey chattered and laughed for a moment, content to sit on his lap but able to reach out and touch Brittany, which she did frequently.

"Well, obviously she's too little for me to talk to," Mrs. Kasey said.

"Oh, I don't know about that," Brittany said. "She talks quite a bit."

"We just don't speak her language," Daniel added.

"Is she standing yet?"

"She pulls herself up on anything she can," Brittany said proudly. "But when she's in a hurry to get somewhere, she crawls like crazy."

"Is she sleeping through the night?"

"Yes. Although I check on her several times during the night," he confessed. "I just need to be sure that she's fine."

Mrs. Kasey nodded and made a notation in her file. "What will you tell her about her parents?"

He blew out a breath. "I didn't know her father, so, hopefully, her grandparents will share that information with her. They instigated this suit without even trying to speak with me. But rest assured, we want them to be a part of her life. They're her family.

"But I can tell her all about her mother. I'll tell her just how sweet and smart Jane was. And how much her mother was loved by everyone who knew her. I'll make sure Hailey knows how much my sister loved her."

Brittany squeezed his hand. "*We'll* make sure she knows that."

A lump materialized in his throat, leaving him unable to speak, so he nodded.

"Would you like to see the rest of the house?" Brittany asked.

"Yes, but first I'd like to see Hailey's room."

"Sure. I'll show you while Daniel gets her snack. She's happy to sit and play for a few minutes after she wakes up, but if she doesn't get her fruit and bottle soon, she's going to raise the roof."

Daniel watched as his wife led the social worker from the room, his heart in his throat and his mind a jumbled mess. There was too much going on for him to process. He hated being out of control of the situation. Being with him was best for Hailey, but he was powerless to make it so.

Not only that, he didn't have power over his emotions or words. What did it mean that he'd had no problem saying he was in love with Brittany? Why had the words felt so right?

Hailey pulled on his ear, reminding him that it was time for her snack, so he went to the kitchen, glad for a moment to get back to his routine and the little he could control.

Relax. Brittany reminded herself that she had been in plenty of tense situations and had never once cracked under the pressure. She wasn't going to start now. But there was no denying this situation was different. Those other times had been business. This was personal. Mrs. Kasey's opinion of her mattered more than winning a contract or pulling off the perfect event. Only her mind and her ego had been involved then. This time, people's hearts were at stake.

"Oh, this is so sweet," the social worker said when she entered Hailey's room.

"Thank you." Brittany had enjoyed decorating the room. Each item had been selected to pique the little girl's curiosity as well as to make her feel special.

Mrs. Kasey picked up the two-sided picture frame on the dresser. On one side, there was a picture of Hailey with her biological parents. On the other, there was a picture of Hailey with Brittany and Daniel. "This is a nice touch. Not everyone would have been so thoughtful."

"We don't want to erase Hailey's past. We just want to assure her future."

"And you think you can do that better than her biological grandparents?"

Brittany met the other woman's eyes. "I don't know them. I'm sure they think they're doing the right thing by fighting for custody. But they're wrong. Daniel is Hailey's father in all the ways that matter."

"And you? Do you consider yourself Hailey's mother?"

"I'm trying to be. She had her biological mother's love for such a short period of time. I know I'll never be able to replace Jane in Hailey's life, but I hope my love will fill her need for a mother's love."

Mrs. Kasey nodded. "You work?"

"Yes."

"Do you intend to continue working outside the home?"

"Yes. Fortunately, Daniel works from home, so he's here for Hailey when I'm not."

Mrs. Kasey's smile broadened. "That's a little unorthodox, but I like the way you think."

"It works for us."

"Not all men would be willing to do that."

"Daniel isn't just any man. He knows who he is and what he wants out of life, but at the same time he wants to make sure that I get what I need to be fulfilled, too. I have no doubt he'll do everything in his power to make sure that Hailey has every opportunity to set and reach her goals, too."

"You sound like you love him."

"I do."

Brittany heard the words but she couldn't believe her ears. The "I do" had just fallen out of her mouth, without her thinking. What did that mean, exactly? Her body started to tremble, from her toes to her hair. Could it be? Could she truly be in love with Daniel?

Her eyes flew back to the social worker. She couldn't let Mrs. Kasey see her nervousness. But the woman merely nodded. Fortunately for Brittany that was the end of the questioning. She was so stunned by her answer and the truth she'd heard there, she didn't know if she could answer any more questions.

She had to take control of herself. She couldn't be in love with Daniel. Theirs was a pretend romance. A marriage on paper. It wasn't the real thing that came complete with emotions and vows that lasted a lifetime.

Daniel had made that clear. It would be foolish of her to pretend otherwise.

Brittany led the way downstairs to the kitchen. As they drew nearer, they could hear Daniel's and Hailey's voices. Daniel was asking Hailey about her favorite toy. She replied in her own language, her voice sincere. Daniel laughed and Hailey echoed him.

Brittany and Mrs. Kasey stepped into the kitchen just as Hailey was finishing her snack. She had banana smeared on her face and bits of Graham cracker on her bib. Daniel was at the sink, wetting a towel. When Hailey saw Brittany, she leaned in her direction and held out her hands.

"Oh, no. Let's get you cleaned up first," Daniel said. He wiped the remnants of Hailey's snack from her face and hands, then removed her bib. Once she was clean, Brittany took her from the high chair and held her. Hailey wrapped her legs around Brittany's waist and leaned against her side.

Mrs. Kasey took in the scene for a moment then spoke. "I think I have all that I need."

"What happens next?" Brittany asked, hiding the anxiety she felt.

"I'll make my report and submit it to the court. It'll be part of the record." Mrs. Kasey looked at them. "I know this is a frustrating procedure and even a little nerve-racking. Just be patient and trust the process. We all want what's best for Hailey."

They thanked Donna Kasey and then walked her to the door and watched as she drove away. Once her car was out of sight, Brittany and Daniel sighed with relief.

"That went well, don't you think?" Daniel asked.

"Yes. And I'm glad it's over."

He put his arm around her shoulder and she leaned against him, grateful for his strength. "You were incredible and very convincing. I don't know how I will ever repay you, but I owe you big-time."

Brittany didn't respond. She couldn't. She'd held it in for the remainder of Mrs. Kasey's visit but now that the pretending was over, she had to admit the truth. To herself anyway.

There was no longer any doubt. She was in love with Daniel.

Obviously, she couldn't tell him. It went against every rule in the deal they'd struck.

No, this was her problem and hers alone. And she'd handle it.

Chapter Seventeen

A few days after the interview with the social worker, Daniel suggested that they get out of the house and have some family fun.

"I don't know. I'm not really in the mood to deal with other people," Brittany said. Though Mrs. Kasey had seemed open-minded, the more Brittany thought about the meeting, the more she wished she had done things differently. What exactly, she wasn't sure. But with nothing but time, she wondered if she should have worn a dress. Or perhaps she should have answered the questions in another way.

Though she'd done her best to be convincing, she couldn't stop worrying that the social worker had seen through her. There was no denying that their marriage had come on the heels of Daniel discovering that Hailey's grandparents wanted custody of her. No denying that they hadn't known each other long before the wedding. Even the most trusting person would be suspicious of the timing. Brittany had barely slept a wink stressing over the entire situation.

But worry over the meeting wasn't the only thing that had kept Brittany awake. Realizing that she was in love with Daniel had had her tossing and turning all night. She was past the point of whining about unrequited love. If nothing else, she was a realist who'd entered into this agreement with her eyes open. Still, knowing that Daniel didn't feel the same hurt. She knew he liked her, that he admired her—he'd told her that often enough. And there was no denying that he was physically attracted to her. But all that didn't equal love.

"Well, I know," Daniel said firmly. "We need to get out of this house. Sitting around and brooding won't change a thing. Besides, I think you were fine. Better than fine. You were awesome."

"Thanks." Maybe he was right. Maybe they needed to get out. "Okay, let's have some fun. And I know the perfect place."

"Where's that?"

"Happy Hearts Animal Rescue."

He nodded. "Sounds good. I'll get Hailey ready."

In minutes, they were in the car and Brittany couldn't stay down in the dumps. Not with a cheerful baby singing in the back seat.

They were a few miles from the rescue when Daniel flashed her a grin. "I was just thinking. Maybe we should get Hailey a puppy."

"Are you kidding?"

"No." He stopped at a red light and then looked over at her again. "From the tone of your voice, I take it you don't think this is a good idea."

"You've got that right. You already have one baby. The last thing you need is a second." He didn't look convinced. The light turned green and he turned his attention back to the road, but she knew he was listening. "Puppies need a lot of love and attention. Like children. At this point, I don't think either of us has the spare energy to give it."

"I have the energy," he said instantly, but his voice lacked conviction.

"Really? Are you hiding it under your bed? Because I haven't seen it."

He laughed and her insides quivered. "Just give me the go-ahead and I'll show you how much energy I have."

Suddenly the air crackled with heat. Suddenly they weren't talking about the puppy any longer. Her body felt damp, but she turned away, not wanting to let him know how hot and bothered she was. Or how tempted she was to give him the go-ahead.

Then he sighed. "I guess you're right. No puppy for now."

His abrupt change back to talking about the puppy was a relief. And a disappointment.

She cleared her throat and pulled herself together. "I know I am. But that doesn't mean Hailey won't have a good time at the rescue. Happy Hearts has a lot of animals that she'll enjoy seeing."

They'd reached the rescue and Daniel turned into the parking lot. Once she was in the stroller and could see all the animals, Hailey began chattering a mile a minute in her secret language.

"You were right," Daniel said. "She's going to enjoy this."

Happy Hearts, which had been started and was run by Daphne Taylor, sat on several lovely acres. The animal rescue was a bone of contention between Daphne and many of her family members. They were cattle ranchers and to them the rescue was an affront and criticism of the family business. Sadly, many other ranchers in the area harbored similar feelings for Daphne, who was only trying to do good. Thanks to her efforts, abandoned or otherwise homeless animals ranging from house pets to horses and goats had a safe home. And since the animals could be adopted, they often found families and forever homes.

Brittany hadn't talked to her friend since the wedding and made a mental note to seek her out. As she recalled the scene between Daphne and her father, her heart ached. Brittany truly hoped that the two of them would reconcile.

"Where should we go first?" Daniel asked.

Brittany looked at Hailey. She was twisting in her seat, straining to get a clear view of the pigs and goats. "I think we have our answer."

They headed down the path to the area where the farm animals were housed. A bunch of little kids swarmed a volunteer who was holding a baby goat. The children jostled and shoved each other in an effort to get closer.

"No need to push," the young woman said firmly. "Everyone is going to get a turn."

Brittany watched as each child took their time petting the goat. When it was Hailey's turn, she kicked her feet and squealed in delight as she rubbed the goat's back. When

Hailey had gotten her fill, Brittany whipped out a baby wipe and cleaned the baby's hands, ignoring her loud protests. No way Hailey was getting sick on her watch.

Next they strolled over to the pigs, where they repeated the process. They encountered some friends and neighbors and stopped to converse. Daniel and Brittany accepted congratulations on their marriage and received invitations to get together in the near future. Then Brittany spotted Daphne in the distance. Although Daphne was smiling, Brittany had a feeling the smile masked an aching heart.

"I'll be back," she said to Daniel. "I want to talk to Daphne."

"Take your time. Hailey and I are going to find the puppies. We'll be there when you finish catching up with your friend."

Brittany quickly walked up to Daphne. "Hey."

Daphne looked up and smiled as Brittany approached. "Hey, newlywed. I'm surprised to see you here. I thought you'd be on your honeymoon."

"With a baby?"

"I imagine that would put a damper on things."

Brittany laughed and looked over at Daniel and Hailey. Daniel caught her eye and smiled at her, pausing momentarily before continuing to the dog barn. Brittany's heart skipped a beat. Realizing she hadn't replied to Daphne's comment, she pulled her eyes away. "Slightly. But Hailey is a real sweetie. I can't imagine life without her."

Daphne poked Brittany's shoulder playfully. "You know, you keep a secret better than anyone I know."

"What do you mean?"

"You and Daniel. I had no idea you were dating. In fact, I didn't know the two of you even knew each other. And the next thing I know, you're married."

Brittany didn't like deceiving her friends and family, but it was necessary. Especially now that the social worker had interviewed her and Daniel. Mrs. Kasey might make her way to friends and family soon. It was better to stick with the story they'd agreed on. "It was a whirlwind affair."

"Yes. But it's obvious that the two of you belong together. The love between you is visible from a mile away."

Brittany's stomach flip-flopped at her friend's words. Though she had begun to face up to her feelings for Daniel, it shocked her to hear someone else remark on them. It was especially jarring when her feelings were growing and becoming stronger each day while Daniel's appeared unchanged. "We're happy together."

"And I'm happy for you both. I don't know Daniel very well, but he seems like a great guy."

"He is," Brittany replied automatically. And honestly.

A volunteer approached, needing to speak with Daphne, so Brittany knew it was time to say goodbye. She hugged her friend. "You're busy. And I'd better get back to Daniel and Hailey."

"Thanks for stopping by. It was good to

talk to you. I hope you and your family have a great time."

Your family. The words echoed through Brittany's head as she walked away to join Daniel and Hailey. Her family.

Daniel and Hailey were watching the puppies tumble over each other as they played. Hailey's happy laughter made it easy for Brittany to find them. When she reached them, Daniel wrapped an arm around her waist, pulling her close. Smiling, she leaned against his side. When Hailey tired of the puppies, they went outside to the dog runs and watched the dogs chase each other. They appeared to be racing, so Brittany cheered on a black Lab that she thought would win.

After a while, Hailey became cranky, so they decided to skip the cat house and call it a day. A quick diaper change and they were on their way back home. Throughout the ride, Daphne's words repeated through Brittany's head. Daniel and Hailey were her family. Those words took on a new meaning now and she knew that whenever this marriage ended, her life would never be the same.

The next days passed in a flurry of activity as Brittany spent hours at the office working on every detail of Daniel's party. She checked and double-checked everything right down to the afternoon of the event. Satisfied, she went home to get ready for the party that evening, looking forward to wearing the new dress and shoes she'd bought for the occasion.

She couldn't stop her mind from racing as she showered and dressed. So much was riding on this dinner. Though Daniel had gotten to know several of her friends over the past few weeks, it was his formal introduction to the community. More importantly, he was going to announce his new venture. Brittany had no doubt that, once people watched the presentation she and Daniel had put together, they would be on board.

Taking a deep breath to calm her nerves, she checked herself one last time in the mirror.

She heard a wolf whistle and turned around.

Daniel leaned against her open doorway and crossed his ankles. Her skin began to tingle as his eyes, alight with desire, traveled over her body. "There are no words to describe just how good you look."

"Thank you." Brittany ran her hand over her formfitting red dress, smoothing out an imaginary wrinkle, and gave him the once-over. Dressed in a navy suit and crisp white shirt with a blue-patterned tie, he was the personification of sexy. "You look pretty snazzy yourself."

He gave her a mischievous look. "I'm ready. Are you?"

Brittany felt her cheeks warm at the double entendre. He'd been a lot more flirtatious the past few days. "I am."

He held out his arm and as she took it, his scent wrapped around her like a lover's embrace. Hailey was spending the night with Brittany's parents so they wouldn't have their tiny chaperone tonight. With Daniel's flirting becoming intense each day and the wall she'd built around her heart weakening with each passing moment, she wondered just what the night would hold for them.

They'd rented DJ's Deluxe again and Brittany's nerves jangled as they neared the restaurant. Daniel parked and they went inside. The guests would be arriving soon and they wanted to be there to greet them.

She'd always had a flair for design and she'd pulled out all the stops to make DJ's even more elegant than it had been for their reception. DJ's waitstaff was top of the line and she knew the service would meet her very high expectations.

She made a quick circuit of the room, checking each centerpiece and place setting to be sure everything was perfect. This event was important to Daniel, but it mattered to her just as much. Her reputation as an event planner would either get a big boost or take a hit, depending on the outcome.

She joined Daniel at the front of the room. He smiled at her and her heart skipped a beat. "Everything up to your standards?"

"Yes."

He took her hand and gave it a gentle squeeze. "Then relax and enjoy yourself."

She smiled at him then turned her focus to the door as the first guests stepped inside—Amanda and her fiancé, Holt. Brittany gave her former roommate a quick hug. "Thanks so much for coming."

"You knew I would be here to support you. Plus, I'm seriously curious about this new secret venture. I believe everyone is." She glanced over her shoulder at Cornelius Taylor, who was standing inside the doorway. "I'd better let you get to it. We'll catch up later."

Cornelius walked up to Brittany and Daniel and looked around. "Very nice."

"My wife planned the entire event," Daniel said. Brittany's heart filled at the pride evident in Daniel's voice. But that was nothing compared to the tingles that raced up and down her spine at his use of the word *wife*. Though she knew they were legally married and nothing else, the sound of the word made her giddy.

"Well, I'm interested to see how it goes.

So far, so good." Cornelius then nodded and walked away.

Daniel wrapped his arm around her shoulders and gave her a squeeze. "By the end of the night, he won't be able to resist your Denim and Diamonds idea."

"I hope so."

Brittany had scheduled everything to the second and, right on time, the waitstaff began circulating with beverages and finger food. Daniel was at his most charming, and the guests responded to his warmth in kind.

At precisely thirty minutes past the hour, dinner was announced. She joined Daniel at their table and looked around. The staff stood in their assigned stations. Brittany signaled and they brought out the first course.

"Everything is great. Relax."

"I want to be sure that everything goes off without a hitch. There's a lot riding on this night." For him and for her.

"Well, you'd better eat or people will start to think there's something wrong with the food."

Brittany laughed. She knew the food was perfect, but she picked up her fork anyway. As she enjoyed her meal, she looked around the room, noting her guests' behavior. If anyone displayed even the slightest bit of unhappiness, she wanted to be able to address it immediately. To her satisfaction, everyone looked happy.

Once dessert and coffee had been enjoyed, Daniel straightened his tie. "Wish me luck."

She caressed his cheek and their eyes met. Held. "You don't need luck. You've got skills."

"Thanks." He kissed her briefly, then rose and went to the front of the room.

"Thank you all for coming tonight. I enjoyed meeting those of you I hadn't met before. I hope to get to know all of you even better in the future. I'd like to spend the next few minutes telling you about the Dubois Guest Ranch and Resort."

He gave a short speech then stepped aside and a short video detailing his upcoming venture played on a wide screen Brittany had set up. When the video ended, the waitstaff passed out glossy brochures containing detailed information. Daniel once more stood in front of the gathering. "It's my belief that the resort will benefit all of Bronco and I welcome discussion on how the resort can further benefit our community. On that note, I'll step aside and let the band play. Please feel free to dance. And of course, I'm available to answer any questions you have."

The applause was thunderous and Brittany was filled with pride. Watching him mingle with their guests, Brittany understood why Daniel had been so successful in business. He was absolutely fantastic, giving each person his undivided attention, listening more than he talked. As much as she wanted to stand around and admire her husband, she still had work to do.

She took two steps and noticed that Cornelius Taylor was walking in her direction. He was smiling broadly and holding a glass of champagne. "This has been an excellent night. I was impressed by your wedding and reception, but this was even more impressive.

I'm rarely wowed, but I was tonight. I want to hire you to organize the Denim and Diamonds fundraiser."

Brittany smiled. "Thank you. You won't be sorry. I have great ideas."

"I'm sure you do. Call my office on Tuesday morning to schedule a meeting."

"Will do."

After that conversation, Brittany practically floated on air. She couldn't wait to share her good news with Daniel. Needing a moment in private to bask in her happiness, she stepped into a secluded alcove. She was there less than a second when Melanie and Gabe happened to step inside.

"Hi," Brittany said. She glanced at Melanie, who looked troubled. "Is something wrong?"

Melanie and Gabe exchanged a look before Melanie answered. "I don't want to be a downer on such a happy occasion."

"Okay, now I'm worried. You two aren't having troubles, are you?"

"No, it's nothing like that," Melanie said.

"It's about Beatrix. I don't think we're ever going to find her."

"Oh. I'm sorry," Brittany said. She knew how important finding Beatrix was to Melanie.

"Don't give up," Gabe said, looking down at his fiancée. "There's still a possibility that something might turn up."

"From where? The only people who responded on the internet were a bunch of frauds or weirdos."

"True. But that doesn't mean the real Beatrix won't reply," Gabe said. "Give it time."

"Gabe's right," Brittany added. "Give it time."

"Time is the one thing we don't have. Winona Cobbs was recently hospitalized—they had to take her to Kalispell. I'm afraid we might lose her before we can tell her that her baby didn't die all those years ago like she'd been led to believe."

"Think positively," Gabe said.

Having nothing to add, Brittany gave her friend a comforting hug before walking away.

She returned to the party and her eyes sought out Daniel. He was standing alone, looking confident and devastatingly handsome and intense longing surged through her. When she joined him, he swept her into his arms and led her to the dance floor. She closed her eyes and placed her head against his muscular chest. If only she could stay in his embrace all night.

After a couple of dances, they reluctantly released each other and made the rounds again. Daniel received many congratulations and requests to discuss his new venture further. Once the last guest had left, Brittany felt safe to say the evening had been a great success.

When they finally arrived home, they looked at each other and grinned. Brittany turned in a circle, her arms over her head. "Yes!"

Daniel took off his jacket and loosened his tie. "That went superbly. Thank you so much for all of your hard work."

Feeling the effects of the champagne she'd

consumed, and buoyed by the success of the night, Brittany smirked. "I told you that I was the best."

"That you are, dear wife. That you are." Daniel pulled her into his arms. "Thank you."

He kissed her lips gently. It was butterfly-soft, but its impact was strong. What was no doubt intended as a simple gesture of gratitude quickly morphed into something else. It was as if a stick of dynamite had been lit inside her and she instantly went up in flames.

Within seconds, the kiss grew more intense. Brittany leaned against his chest, needing to get closer. He started to pull away, so she wrapped her arms around his neck, pulling him back to her. The weeks of simmering desire had boiled over and she didn't want to control it. Being kissed by Daniel felt terrific and she didn't want it to end.

He kissed her a moment longer, as if his emotions were as out of control as hers, then gradually pulled back and leaned his forehead against hers. She was breathing heavily and it took a moment for her heart to slow down.

"I'm sorry," he said. The guilt written on his face also dripped from his voice. "That was entirely inappropriate."

"Don't apologize. I liked it."

"But we have a deal. We agreed our marriage would be in name only."

"I know. But this is what I want now."

"And later?"

"Later can take care of itself."

"Are you sure?"

"Yes."

He kissed her again. Then he pulled back and offered her his hand. There would be no "getting carried" up the stairs tonight. She had to walk into his bedroom, removing any lingering doubt that she wanted to make love with him.

Her heart thudded loudly in her chest and her blood pulsed through her veins as desire and excitement filled her. With each step, the longing and need expanded inside her. By the time they reached his bedroom, Brittany thought she would explode. She reached up, removed his loosened tie and draped it over a chair, then began to unbutton his shirt. He returned the favor, unzipping her dress.

When they were both undressed, they fell onto the king-size bed. Brittany might not have been ready to put her feelings into words, but she wasn't shy about showing Daniel just how she felt.

This was what had been missing from their relationship. Now their marriage was complete.

After making love with Daniel, she didn't think she would be able to go back to a marriage of convenience. Nor would she want to. The question was—did he feel the same?

Chapter Eighteen

Daniel stretched and looked down at his wife, who was snuggled close to his side. Last night had been the best of his life. It was as if every dream he'd ever had, and some he hadn't, had come true. Brittany was a generous lover. Given the nature of their relationship—their marriage was a business arrangement, after all—he'd expected her to be a little bit shy. He'd been wrong. She hadn't been the least bit bashful. They'd made love all night, until the wee hours of the morning, and Brittany had been a confident lover. They'd fit together so perfectly, it was as if she'd been created especially for him.

After a moment, guilt began to poke holes in his joy, and the sense of well-being began to seep away. How would Brittany react today? Would she be happy or filled with regret? Last night they'd been swept away by the success of the event. Everyone had been enthusiastic about his plan and Brittany had landed the account she'd worked so hard to get. They'd been flying high. Mix in the champagne they'd consumed and it was easy to see how they'd ended up making love all night.

The night was over and the sun was rising. Brittany would be waking soon. She'd already begun to stir, so it would soon be time to face the music. He didn't know how she would feel in the cold light of day, so he'd watch her closely and pick up on her mood. Hopefully, by following her lead, he'd say the right thing.

He didn't delude himself into believing that one night spent making love would change the course of her life. She'd been clear that she didn't want to be a mother. And he had Hailey, so that ruled him out as playing a permanent role in her life. If he'd even dared to hope the past weeks together had changed her mind about the kind of future she wanted, her joy at landing the Taylor account killed that hope. Brittany had the right to create the kind of life she wanted. If she wanted to live her life without children, then she should. Sadly, that meant they had no future together. But Daniel refused to make her feel guilty about her choices. She'd upheld her end of the bargain. She didn't owe him anything else. He wouldn't try and hold onto her no matter how desperately he wanted to.

But she was here now, and he intended to make the most of the time he had. Her eyes opened and she looked at him. Though he tried, he couldn't decipher the expression on her face. Her lovely brown eyes were unreadable. That meant he couldn't tell whether she regretted last night or if her body was still humming with contentment as his was.

Before he could decide what to say, his phone rang. He picked it up immediately.

"Hello?"

"Daniel, it's John Kirkland." His lawyer's normally calm voice sounded excited.

"What's up? Do you have news about the case? Have you seen the social worker's report?"

Brittany's eyes widened and she sat up, pulling the sheet over her perfectly round breasts and momentarily distracting him.

"No. It won't matter now anyway."

"Why won't it matter?"

"What's happening?" Brittany asked.

Realizing she had nearly as much at stake as he did, Daniel put the phone on speaker so she could hear, too.

"I just received word that the Larimars have withdrawn their custody suit."

"Say that again," Daniel said. His head was spinning. Despite the fact that Brittany had just let out a joyous cheer, he couldn't believe his ears.

John laughed. "You heard me. They're no

longer trying to take Hailey from you. I'm going to make a motion asking the judge to grant you permanent wardship and custody of Hailey. And I advise you to proceed with your plans to adopt her as soon as possible to prevent anything else like this from happening again. But it's over."

"So that's it. They disrupt my life, threaten Hailey's security, and then drop everything. No apology. No nothing." Daniel was at once angry and grateful. He expected he'd run the whole gamut of emotions before the end of the day.

"Why? Why are they dropping the suit now after putting me through all this? It doesn't make sense."

"Apparently, Mrs. Larimar was recently diagnosed with cancer and her husband doesn't feel capable of raising a baby right now."

"I see."

"I'll forward the documents. Congratulations again."

"Wait," Daniel said abruptly before his attorney could hang up. He exhaled the bitterness he felt. Hailey's happiness was still his number one priority. "If they want to maintain contact with Hailey, they can. We can arrange visitation in the future. In the meantime, I'll bring Hailey to visit them if Mrs. Larimar is up to it."

"I'll pass on your offer and get back to you."

Daniel ended the call and turned to Brittany. Her bright smile was a balm to his soul. "I'm so happy for you, Daniel. And for Hailey, too. You're a family and you're going to stay together. You should be happy."

"I am happy." He noticed that she'd excluded herself from the family. She was already distancing herself from them. Perhaps she was mentally returning to her regularly scheduled life.

"You don't look happy."

"I am. I was angry for a second, but I'm not anymore," he insisted.

"That's good. But something else is wrong. I can tell."

"It's just…" He blew out a breath.

"Just what?"

"This is another loss for Hailey. I don't know the kind of cancer her grandmother has or her prognosis, but that's one more person she can potentially lose."

"That's not necessarily so. People are surviving cancer these days. She could live for a very long time and be a positive part of Hailey's life."

He nodded. Naturally, Brittany would think of something that hadn't occurred to him. "True."

An awkward silence settled over them and he searched for something to say. Before he could find a subject, Brittany spoke.

"So, I guess that's the end of things for us. Now that you aren't at risk of losing custody of Hailey, you don't need me anymore."

He didn't need her anymore? He only wished that were true. In the short time they'd been married, he'd grown close to her. He enjoyed every moment they spent together and had anticipated sharing many more in the future. After last night, he'd begun to hope theirs would become a marriage in every sense of the word. That hope was now completely dashed. Brittany wanted out.

He could tell her that he wanted her to stay, but he wouldn't. He knew her too well. He knew she might stay for his and Hailey's sakes, sacrificing what she wanted to keep him happy. That wouldn't be fair.

Not only that, he could ask her to stay and she could say no and leave. She had every right. There was no need to open himself up for the agony such a rejection would bring. His heart had been battered enough in this lifetime. It had hurt to be rejected by a sister he'd loved so much, devastating to be shut out of her life only to lose her forever. And he was still recovering from the loss of his parents. He couldn't open his heart again when he knew it could be pummeled.

Oh, he was sure Brittany would do her best to let him down easy—she was too sweet to do anything else. But she was also too honest to pretend to want a life with him when she didn't. And he wasn't going to put her in a position that would leave both of them uncomfortable. So he decided to tell her the part of the truth that didn't leave him open to hurt and that would set her free at the same time.

"I will never be able to thank you enough for what you've done. Though our marriage is ending a lot more quickly than either of us anticipated, I hope that you'll stay in our lives. Hailey really does love you."

He was wrong when he thought that would save him from being hurt. The pain of those words nearly undid him.

Hailey really does love you. Brittany had to give him credit for being subtle. His statement of Hailey's feelings with no mention of his own might as well have been yelled from the rooftop. She heard him loud and clear. Daniel didn't love her and was too considerate to utter the words. Not that the situation required he make such a declaration. She'd gone into this marriage knowing that it would be in name only. The fact that they'd somehow ended up making love last night didn't change the agreement or his feelings, obviously.

Though she was disappointed and maybe even a little bit hurt, she understood. He might have made love to her with such tenderness that she'd begun dreaming of a future where their vows become real, but wanting something to be true didn't make it so. And he'd been very clear from the beginning why he'd wanted to marry her. A future with her wasn't one of them. Since she'd insisted that their marriage be in name only and end once he'd gotten custody, she had no right to be upset that he wanted to stick to the terms.

She might want to see if their marriage could last, but that was her problem. She wasn't going to try to change his mind or to make him feel guilty. She was a big girl and would act like one.

She pulled the sheet higher on her chest and wiggled up on her pillow. "I enjoyed myself. And, of course, I'll keep in touch. Hailey is important to me, too."

She hadn't been the least bit self-conscious

last night, but now she was uncomfortably aware that she and Daniel were completely naked beneath the sheet. The dress she'd worn to the party was on the floor in a puddle of red silk. She couldn't reach it without getting out of bed and baring her nude body was out of the question now. But she couldn't lie there so close to him that she inhaled his masculine scent with every breath. The heat of his body had her longing to get closer, but she wouldn't. Last night's sweet magic was gone, leaving only the bitter taste of disappointment behind.

Daniel stared off into the distance, as if lost in thought. Perhaps he'd moved on mentally and had already forgotten she was there. But he was the one with a robe on the foot of the bed, not her. Well, since he didn't seem inclined to move, she scooted to the edge of the bed and managed to grab his robe without revealing too much of herself. Not that he was looking.

Once she'd put on his robe, she stood and tied the belt around her waist before glancing at him. His eyes were a mixture of humor and confusion. Apparently, she hadn't been as graceful or inconspicuous in real life as she'd been in her mind.

"I think I'll shower and get dressed. Then I guess we can go to my parents' house and get Hailey."

He nodded.

"Then I'll come back here and pack. Good thing we didn't bring everything I own."

"There's no hurry, Brittany. It's not as if I'm evicting you."

"Maybe not, but there's no reason to draw things out unnecessarily, either. Besides, my place is a lot closer to my office. Now that I've landed the Taylor account, I'll be super busy. I'll need the extra time I'll save on the commute."

His eyes narrowed and, for a minute, she thought she'd seen pain flash in them. But then he smiled and she knew she'd imagined it. Why would he feel anything remotely resembling pain? He'd gotten everything he'd wanted and, as far as he was concerned, the contract had been fulfilled. No need to prolong the inevitable goodbye.

"Okay, then," he said. "I guess I need to shower and get dressed myself."

"I'll bring back your robe in a little while."

"Sure."

With that awkward conversation now over, Brittany gathered her discarded clothes and shoes and then went to her room. When the door was firmly closed behind her, she sat on the bed and ordered herself not to cry. There was no reason for her heart to be breaking. No reason at all. But then, love wasn't ruled by reason.

Chapter Nineteen

Daniel walked past the now empty bedroom for the umpteenth time. Brittany had been gone for five days, but he still missed her like crazy. The hint of her perfume lingered in the air, making him long for her even more. She'd forgotten one of her scarves and he'd placed it in his sock drawer where he saw it every morning. He knew he was being ridiculous and that he should return it to her, but that scrap of silk made him feel closer to her.

He shouldn't have let her go. But what choice had he had? She didn't want a family. She'd been clear about that. Brittany had married him for the money that he'd promised to give her so she could start her own event planning company. She'd lit out of here so fast he hadn't had the chance to hand her the check he'd written for the agreed-upon amount. When he'd noticed it on his desk two days later, he'd torn it up, filled out a check for twice the amount and dropped it in the mail. He could have delivered it to her in person, but he was afraid if he saw her, he might beg her to come back to him.

Hailey began rousing from her nap and he went to her nursery so he'd be there when she was fully awake. He stood by her crib, wishing that Brittany was there beside him as she'd been over the past weeks. Though he had Hailey, his heart still ached from loneliness. And unrequited love.

He sucked in a breath and was momentarily dizzy. What? Had he just thought that he was in love with Brittany? He couldn't be. But as he pondered the words, the truth sank in and he couldn't avoid it. *He was in love with Brit-*

tany. He probably had been for quite some time. He'd just been too blind to see it.

But in his defense, it had happened so gradually, he hadn't noticed when his feelings changed. One minute he'd thought her a competent employee. Then he'd thought of her as a friend. And, finally, a lover. She was beautiful, so his attraction hadn't been unexpected. But love? That had caught him off guard and he hadn't known what name to give it. And now it was too late.

He'd been so sure his growing feelings would disappear if she wasn't around. Instead he found himself prowling the house as if she would magically materialize in the family room. Or better yet, in his bed. The night they'd made love had been more than he could ever imagine, and he wanted to duplicate it every night for the rest of his life.

It had almost killed him to let her go. Standing by silently with a fake smile on his face while she'd packed her belongings, and then helping her load his SUV so she could leave him, had been a colossal mistake. But what was he supposed to do? She was the one who'd said it was time to leave the morning after they'd made love. The night that had changed everything for him hadn't affected her at all.

The phone had still been in his hand when she'd announced that she was leaving him. She'd made up some lame excuse about her condo being closer to her job and then turned her back on him. She'd said he'd gotten everything he'd wanted. The truth was, she'd gotten everything she'd wanted. Or she would have, the minute she cashed the check.

He fought against the bitterness welling inside him. Brittany hadn't done anything wrong. In fact, she'd given more than she'd agreed to. Falling in love hadn't been a part of it. Nor had staying with him. So he shouldn't be upset that she'd gone.

Once he'd changed Hailey's diaper, he carried her downstairs and gave her a snack. He hadn't tried to find a new nanny since Brittany had left. Instead, he'd made room for Hailey in his office. He'd brought in a playpen and some of her favorite toys so she could play while he worked. He wasn't as productive as he'd been when he'd had help, but he enjoyed her company. Now, after settling her in the playpen, he picked up the mail.

He tossed aside the junk mail and then looked at the envelope addressed in his own hand. The check he'd sent to Brittany. She'd written "Return to Sender" and sent it back unopened. That didn't make sense. The money was his part of the bargain. She'd earned it. She needed it to start her business. Yet she'd sent it back to him. What did that mean? Why would she toss away the opportunity to make her dream a reality?

Daniel set the check aside and continued to go through the mail. After reading and rereading a three-paragraph letter without being able to comprehend a word, he knew it was futile to continue. His mind was too filled with thoughts of Brittany for him to focus.

He'd always been able to think clearly when riding a horse. Unfortunately, given that he had yet to put Hailey on a horse with him, and there was no one she was comfortable with enough to watch her, that was out of the question. So he did the next best thing. He called Stephanos. His best friend possessed the ability to help him see things he couldn't see.

Once he'd reached Stephanos and explained the situation, Daniel listened for what seemed like forever while his friend laughed. He was starting to regret calling him and was in the middle of saying so when his friend spoke.

"I don't know what you want me to say," Stephanos said once his laughter had died down.

"I don't know, either, but I certainly didn't expect you to laugh at me."

"I always laugh at the ridiculous. You know that."

"What's so ridiculous?"

"This whole thing. You marry a woman you don't love—a woman you barely know—because you're worried about losing Hailey. Then it turns out that you don't need to be married, after all, so she leaves. And now you're upset with her. Am I missing anything?"

"No."

Stephanos laughed again. "Oh, I think I am."

"What?"

"The fact that you've fallen in love with your wife and are too scared to let her know."

"I'm not scared." He just didn't want to put Brittany in a bad spot.

"Tell that to someone who doesn't know you as well as I do."

Daniel dropped his head into his hands. He should have known better than to call Stephanos. They'd been friends too long to be able to deceive each other. "What should I do?"

"I can't believe you're asking me that."

"Neither can I."

Stephanos laughed again and Daniel seriously considered finding a new best friend. "It's easy. Go get your woman."

Go get your woman. That thought stuck with Daniel throughout the rest of the day. It echoed through his mind as he tried to sleep that night. *Go get your woman* was the first thing he thought of the next morning. And though he'd been hesitant at first, by the time he'd finished giving Hailey her breakfast, he knew what he had to do.

Brittany sat on the sofa and adjusted the pillow behind her back yet again. Though the condo had felt like home from the day she'd moved in, she felt out of place. The bed she'd slept in until she'd moved in with Daniel no longer felt familiar. While in the past she'd rested easily, she now tossed and turned all night and woke with a feeling of unrest that followed her throughout the day.

She'd managed to get started on the Denim and Diamonds fundraiser for Cornelius Taylor. While she was excited about the possibilities the future held for her professionally, she was no longer certain about the direction of her personal life. Even though marriage and children hadn't been part of her life plan, being with Daniel and Hailey had

changed her. She suddenly felt herself longing for her husband and child. Their relationship might have been short, but it had been
wonderful. What had started out as a pretend
marriage had turned into a marriage so real
she couldn't even think about its loss without crying.

Whenever she felt weak and considered returning to the ranch, one thing held her in
place. Daniel didn't want her. He'd been almost cheerful as he'd helped her move back
into the condo. She'd half expected him to
dance a jig on the way to his SUV after he'd
carried in the last box. And all the while her
heart had been breaking. But she'd kept it together and had given him her best smile.

She didn't know how long she would be
able to keep up the act. No one at work knew
her marriage had ended. Every day she pretended to be a happy newlywed. Amanda
knew something was up, but she hadn't asked
questions. She'd simply let Brittany know
she was there if she wanted to talk. Worse,
she hadn't told her family the truth, either.

They still had the impression that she and Daniel were together. She knew she needed to come clean and stop living a lie, but she couldn't. But not just because of her pride. To do so would mean accepting that her marriage was over and the man she loved didn't love her in return. She wasn't ready to face that yet.

One thing was certain. She couldn't continue to live in the condo. It no longer felt like home. Now it felt like failure. Sadly the ranch that felt like home would never be home again.

There was a knock on her door and she forced herself to her feet. Though she wasn't in the mood to deal with anyone, she was sick of her own company, too.

"Coming," she called when the knock came again. Apparently, her uninvited guest was anxious to see her.

She ran a hand over her hair, then glanced through the peephole. Her mouth fell open. *Daniel.* She hurriedly unlocked and opened the door. "Hi."

"I need to talk to you."

He seemed panicked and her heart skipped a beat. "Where's Hailey? Is she okay?"

"She's fine. I dropped her at your parents' house before I came here. She could do with a little spoiling today." He shifted his feet and shoved his hands into his pockets. "Can I come in?"

"What? Oh, sure."

"Thanks."

She led him to the living room and they sat on the sofa. He didn't speak, and with every passing second she grew more uneasy.

Was he here to talk about getting a divorce? Perhaps he'd already hired an attorney—something she hadn't been able to bring herself to do—and wanted to tell her in person. She searched for something to say to break the silence. "Would you like something to drink?"

"No, thanks." He looked around and she got the feeling he wasn't seeing her condo but was rather using the time to gather his thoughts. He didn't seem his usual confident self. "I guess I should just get to the point."

She nodded.

"I made a mistake and I need your help. You're the only one who can help me fix it."

"Okay." Her heart sank as she realized she'd hoped that he'd come here for personal reasons. Instead, it was business. Thank goodness she hadn't said or done anything to let him know how she felt. That would be too embarrassing for her to ever live down. "How can I help?"

He rubbed his hands over his denim-clad thighs. "I—" He cleared his throat. Obviously he was nervous which only made her more uncomfortable. She needed him to spit it out already before she lost what little composure she had.

Daniel inhaled and blew out his breath then spoke quickly, the words running together. "I made a mistake and let someone that I love walk away."

"What?" He'd spoken so quickly Brittany wasn't sure what he'd said.

He sighed and looked her in the eyes. The emotion she saw there made her heart skip a beat. "I said, I made a mistake when I let you go without telling you that I love you. I should have told you the morning after we made love, but you wanted to leave, and I knew it would be unfair to hold you. But I do love you, Brittany."

Her heart began to soar.

"I know that marriage and motherhood weren't in your plans," he continued. "And I've tried to respect that and let you live the life you chose. The thing is, I can't live without you."

"What?" Brittany knew she was repeating herself, but she couldn't believe what she was hearing. Did he really mean it?

"I love you."

The simply spoken vow healed the hurt that had been piercing her heart ever since they'd parted.

"You're right, Daniel. I never planned on getting married and having children. My career was all I'd needed. All I'd imagined wanting." The hope in his eyes faded and he stiffened, seeming to withdraw into himself. She realized how easily a carelessly spoken word could hurt him which was the last thing she'd ever want to do. "But that all changed when I married you and became Hailey's mother. Then I realized there was room in my life and my heart for more than a career."

His eyes warmed and his smile grew as she spoke. "Does that mean you'll consider giving us a second chance? I'll do the best that I can to be a good husband and show my love to you every minute of every day. Do you think you might want to try being married again? For real this time."

"Yes! Oh, yes."

They reached for each other and kissed. The love she'd been feeling for him filled her heart to overflowing. The life that she'd planned was nice, but it was no longer the one she wanted. Now she wanted a life that included Daniel and Hailey and the love they'd found.

They joined hands and walked to her bedroom together. She had a feeling that her bed was going to be a lot more comfortable with him in it.

Epilogue

November...

Daniel stepped into the front room, then stopped and looked at Brittany and Hailey. The two special women in his life were playing with one of Hailey's favorite toys, the plastic doughnuts. Brittany held up the rings one at a time and told Hailey the color. Hailey babbled or laughed in return.

The past few weeks had been the best of his life. Once he and Brittany had confessed their love for each other and pulled down the walls that they'd each been holding up, their marriage had become even better than he'd ever dreamed. Every day was happier than the one before.

As planned, Brittany had started working on a business plan for her own event planning business. For now, she was busy at Bronco Elite, but eventually she wanted to be ready to go her own way.

She'd been working diligently on the upcoming Denim and Diamonds fundraiser, which would take place in two weeks. Cornelius Taylor had been thrilled by her proposals and had been singing her praises far and wide. Brittany was well on her way.

Brittany looked up as he entered the room. The radiance of her smile rivaled that of the sun. He couldn't believe his luck in finding her.

"How did the fence repairing go?" she asked, standing and giving him a hug.

"Fine. It feels good to be back working the ranch."

"Even with the resort guests?"

He laughed. "We'll see. The first guests won't be arriving for a few more weeks."

They returned to where the baby played and sat back down. He set Hailey on his lap.

"How do you feel about tomorrow?" Brittany asked.

"I'm excited. And a little bit nervous." The Larimars were coming for a weeklong visit tomorrow. He and Brittany had been in touch with them ever since the older couple had dropped the custody suit. They spoke on the phone regularly. Daniel had offered to bring Hailey to see them, but they'd preferred coming to Montana. Daniel had a feeling they wanted to see where Hailey was living. Best of all, the social worker had filed her report approving Hailey's adoption by Daniel and Brittany.

"They're going to love you," she said, cupping his cheek.

He turned his face, kissing her palm. "*Us.* They're going to love us."

The doorbell rang and he gave her Hailey and then jumped to his feet. A minute later he returned to the room. "What's behind your back?" Brittany asked as she stood up, Hailey in her arms.

He revealed a bouquet of red roses. "It occurred to me that I've never brought you flowers or given you gifts."

She kissed Hailey's forehead. "I beg to differ."

His heart warmed knowing that she considered Hailey a gift. Of course, she'd proved that several times over these past weeks. Together they'd managed to balance work and caring for Hailey.

"I guess it's more accurate to say that I didn't woo you. Our marriage began as a business arrangement. We fell in love, but that doesn't change the way things started. I know our marriage is real, but I want to do some of the things I would have done if we'd had a more traditional beginning. I would have courted you. I would have given you flowers and candy. I would have taken you out to dinner. Bought you jewelry. You deserve those things."

Brittany stood on her tiptoes and brushed a kiss against his lips. Her lips lingered against his, giving him a taste of what he would enjoy that night. Anticipation was a wonderful thing.

"Thank you."

He handed her the bouquet and she handed Hailey to him. She sniffed the roses and closed her eyes for a moment, as if in bliss.

"You're welcome."

Brittany smiled at Hailey and pointed at Daniel. "Who's that wonderful man?"

Hailey looked from Brittany to Daniel. Then she grinned and said clearly, "Dada."

* * * * *

LET'S TALK
Romance

For exclusive extracts, competitions
and special offers, find us online:

f facebook.com/millsandboon

⊙ @millsandboonuk

🐦 @millsandboon

Or get in touch on 0844 844 1351*

For all the latest titles coming soon,
visit millsandboon.co.uk/nextmonth

*Calls cost 7p per minute plus your phone company's price per
minute access charge